The Robbie Burns Revival
&
Other Stories

The Robbie Burns Revival & Other Stories by Cecilia Kennedy © 2004.

Several of these stories have previously appeared in *Storyteller Magazine* and *The Grist Mill*.

Editor for the press, Richard Cumyn.
Cover photo: "Robert Burns 200 Celebration, Dumfries, Scotland" © Joe Blades 1996.
Design and in-house editing by the publisher, Joe Blades.
Printed and bound in Canada by Sentinel Printing, Yarmouth NS.

The publisher acknowledges the support of the Canada Council for the Arts and the New Brunswick Culture and Sport Secretariat-Arts Development Branch.

Broken Jaw Press Inc.
Box 596 Stn A   **www.brokenjaw.com**
Fredericton NB E3B 5A6   jblades@brokenjaw.com
Canada   tel / fax 506 454-5127

National Library of Canada Cataloguing in Publication Data

Kennedy, Cecilia, 1953-
    The Robbie Burns revival & other stories / Cecilia Kennedy.

ISBN 1-55391-024-9

    I. Title.

PS8571.E62735R62 2004   C813'.6   C2004-900668-1

The Robbie Burns Revival

Other Stories

Cecilia Kennedy

Fredericton • Canada

Acknowledgements:

Many patient people provided helpful information and technical advice for these stories. They include: Balfour Legresley whose family brought the original Yorkshire violets to Canada; RCMP Corporal Orest Hnatikiw; Richard Soo SJ; Nadia Kowalyshyn, Daniel and Vera Geraghty who introduced me to the pleasure of Burns Night; Ontario Justice of the Peace Olli Dignard, and Richard Feltoe of the Upper Canada Living History Association. I am grateful to the following writers for helpful criticism and fellowship: Barry Fluxgold, J.W. Parker, Herbert Batt, Sylvia Maultash Warsh, and Melanie Fogel, the excellent editor of *Storyteller Magazine.* My family (Byron, Mary-Catharine, Cyril, Theodora, Columba and Aidan) have been my first readers, have indulged my escapes into Tony's world, and have been a constant support: *thank you.*

The Robbie Burns Revival
&
Other Stories

For my parents
Agatha Huitenga & Walter Pieterse
who taught me to love a good story.

Flowers of Yorkshire

My first posting. "This is Constable Tony Aardehuis," said Sergeant Willis, introducing the rookie to the detachment at Port Rose. Like always, my Dutch name, supposed to rhyme with "paradise", melted down fast. Willis, doing his best, said, "Ardhoos."

He gave me a locker next to a thickset man with a grizzled brush cut and a badger brush moustache. "Need any advice, ask Ted Gorman. He knows more about running this place than I do."

"Damn right." Gorman smiled for the sergeant, and crushed my hand.

At the college they'd warned us expect some haze in the air of our first posting, so I wasn't surprised when my shoes disappeared and reappeared, or I showed up for a duty printed only on my copy of the schedule, or when my name kicked around the staff room like a tin can: Arduous, Arthose …

"What's it mean?" asked Sergeant Willis after a few days.

"House of earth."

"Outhouse," laughed one of the guys.

"Shithouse," said Ted Gorman.

Most of it was dumb fun that waned by the end of the first few weeks. Except for Gorman.

Even though Port Rose was the first detachment east of Toronto it was small town enough to run a piece on the new constable in the weekly *Enterprise & Courier*. Tony Aardehuis, Eastern Ontario farmboy, joins the OPP after stints as dairyman, typing teacher, farm implement salesman. "Took a while to figure out what I wanted. Now I have," says the young constable. The killer: graduate of the University of Ottawa. Fifteen courses in English, History and Philosophy — I might as well have sat in Gorman's chair.

"Hey, Shithouse," he said the next morning, "Shithouse, B.A. Stands for bare ass, right? How far you have to bend?"

I stopped buttoning my jacket to stare at him. I had a few inches on him; he had shoulders like a truck. I was on probation. He was not. "What the hell are you on about?" I said.

"This, you fast-tracking little shit." He tapped his years-of-service badge. Twenty-five years and still a constable. He leaned close, demanding a reaction.

"Heads up," said one of the guys. "Sergeant's coming."

After that, Gorman never let up. Six months of coffee spills, porn to-make-you-vomit dropped on my desk, screw-ups with files and phone messages. He never let up and he never pushed past the point where easy going Sergeant Willis would have to sit on him. I figured eventually he'd tire of the game, or clue in that I was just a mild mannered boy from Armagh, Ontario, or my time on this posting would run out.

One late April afternoon I was working counter beside Sergeant Willis when Gorman stomped into the detachment shoving a lurching old man in front of him, cuffs on so tight they cut deep into the wrinkled wrists.

"One hundred acres, the east half of lot 11, concession five west of the Port Rose line ..." said the scrawny old guy, his beat-up barn clothes steaming with the ripe smell of cow manure. He struggled in Gorman's grip, chanting the property description like a prayer, "One hundred acres, the east half of lot eleven ..."

"Shut up." Gorman shoved him hard against the counter, glanced at Willis. "He's at it again. The old bastard just sprayed the **Member of Provincial Parliament**'s office with a load of manure. A half-ton of cow shit dumped on the sidewalk downtown. Got the crap all over my shoes."

Willis sighed and talked to the prisoner like he was dealing with a child, "I thought we were done with all this, Garnet."

The prisoner's John Deere cap was on crooked, the lines cut deep in his face. He could look like a scrawny clown, except for the clear blue eyes that glared at Willis, unwavering. "It's my land."

Willis sighed again. "Take him down, Tony."

"Go for it, farmboy. The stink'll make you feel right at home."

"Cut it out, Gorman," said the sergeant.

Later, Willis told me Garnet Robson's story. He'd been just another farmer, milking cows on land owned by his family for a century or more until the province, hunting for a place to put Toronto's garbage, settled on a quadrant of dense clay basin in Giller Township as the perfect site. Five years ago the farms of Garnet Robson and four others had been expropriated.

"Course they fought it, tooth and nail. Course they lost. The others, they took the settlement money, bought new farms, moved on. But Garnet Robson went right off the deep end. I don't know why. Yeah, his family's been on that piece of dirt for a long time, but it's not like he had any kids to leave the place to."

"Off the deep end?"

"The bottle, mostly. We've had him in for drunk and disorderly. Harassing the bureaucrats. There's a restraining order on him for the Waste Authority Office — can't go within 50 metres of the place. And trespass on his farm."

He corrected himself. "What used to be his farm. Last year he set out to do his spring plowing like usual. Finally they put an eight foot fence around the whole site. I wish they'd just get on with it. Open the big hole in the ground and start trucking the crap in. It breaks his heart to see the land lying there, waiting. But they're s'posed to start digging next month."

Willis smiled ruefully and shook his head. "Guess I should'a expected a last little flurry from old Garnet."

When I took his dinner down Robson still smelled like an alcoholic barn but he eyed the bowl of microwave soup and grilled cheese sandwich with mild interest.

He took a long slurping sip of the coffee and gave me a once over with a pair of piercing blue eyes. "Why'd he call you farmboy?"

"What?"

"That snake who brought me in, he called you farmboy."

"My dad farms. Other side of Kingston."

"Dairy?"

I nodded. "Guernsey herd. Him and my brother, they milk about 50."

"I had Ayreshires." Clearly he'd decided I belonged to his world; we might have been chatting at the stock barn on sale day, so I sat down across from him on the empty bunk.

"Not too many of them around."

"No. But Ayreshires is what we always had. Brought the first bull to Upper Canada in 1837," he said with pride while he spooned the soup with a crack-nailed hand, as gnarled and tough as my dad's. He told me how the first Robsons had come from Yorkshire 200 years ago, looking for stoneless fields and a fairer shake.

"Must'a been hard," I said, trying to plant some seeds that might keep him out of this cell in the future, "but sometimes you have to do that. Move on. Start over in a new place."

But he didn't get my meaning, or didn't want to. "Oh, they were homesick. One girl, Jane Robson, sent for these flowers from home, pining for the sight of something from the old country. Planted them behind the house. Violets still blooming, you know, every May, have a nice light smell. For a while the wife and I tried hard to find out what kind they were but no one seemed to know. Be blooming next month. Always was a special place there, under the birches."

All of a sudden he put the bowl of soup down so hard it splashed onto his knees and he said, "My God, I wonder if there's anything left?"

Left to live for? Left of those violets? I didn't point out that next month it would hardly matter what was left under those birches. Jane Robson's flowers and Garnet's history would be buried under the first layers of a hill of garbage.

Then Garnet Robson looked hard at the white wall above my head and the conversation took a sharp bend. "Your father, he's damn lucky. Two sons, one working with him."

"Yes."

"I had a boy."

I remembered what Willis had said about Robson having no kids and the surprise must have shown on my face.

Garnet smiled sadly. "Oh, he didn't live. Born way too soon. Months too soon, but not so's you couldn't tell he was a boy. Them days, there was nothing could be done and the wife had no more after him."

Garnet Robson was a sad old story and I couldn't help wondering how my feisty dad would fare against the same fates. He'd crossed his own ocean and had his own lost children — including a miscarriage buried in the apple orchard. That happened before I was born in the days when a family quietly took care of such matters itself. I only knew about it at all because my big brother Mike, who'd watched through a hedge, for some strange reason had to tell me about it the night his Jonas was born. As if he needed finally to offload the mix of terror and pity that twists inside a boy who sees his stern father digging the earth with fierce blows, burying a small box, crying as he sets a handful of apple blossoms on the place.

But in spite of ups and downs my dad wound down his life secure in his acres, wife and family around him. Garnet Robson ended alone, even his land lost, even the clumps of flowers that tied him to his past. Not fair. Not fair at all. And those flowers reminded me of my mother, and a plot of blazing orange tulips nursed with the same care she gave to opening air mail letters from Holland.

So I spent my break with the old man. We talked breeds and milk production, the impact of GATT, the future of milk marketing boards, and slowly the bend in his shoulders eased.

Every hour for the rest of the shift Willis said, "Tony, go check on the old guy."

I'd dimmed the lights as much as I could but the old guy lay either wakeful and talking to himself, or sleeping and mumbling in his dreams. All night I heard the rasp of his voice, winnowing dry old words in the dark. The lost land. Fields planted in such and such a year with such and such a crop. His wife stitching in the lamplight for a lost child.

"Made a quilt for the boy. Going to call him Joseph. Blue sailboats with red pennants."

Then Garnet's ragged mind veered toward barn building or how a girl named Jane Robson brought violets from Yorkshire. "Planted under the birches. Bloom in May with a sweet scent light on the evening air ..."

The next day Garnet Robson was out on bail, his tractor and manure wagon impounded, the MPP's office added to the restraining order. So I didn't see him again till a month later, the May afternoon before digging was set to start on the new dump. Gorman brought him into the detachment again, shoved him, again, hard into the counter.

"Caught the old bugger at the fence."

Reeking of 40-proof, Robson struggled against the cuffs. "Just looking through a fence. Can't a man look at a fence?"

"Shit, Garnet, I wish you'd get over it," sighed Willis and turned to grab an incident report. While his back was turned Gorman gave a vicious twist to the old man's arm.

I asked, "Did he have wire cutters on him?"

Gorman stared. "No."

"So what's the charge gonna be?" I asked, in my best rookie cop just-trying-to-learn-the-ropes voice.

"Trespass."

"But I didn't do no trespass," said Garnet, not so drunk he couldn't take a serve. "I was on the outsidda the fence."

Thoughtful, Willis put his pencil down.

"Drunk and disorderly then."

"I may be drunk but how's it disorderly for a man to have a last look at his place? Through a fence."

Gorman's eyes were slits in his greasy face. "Driving impaired."

Robson drew himself up straight. "I didn't drive. I walked."

"Alright," Willis sighed, "I can't arrest you for impaired walking. Get outta here and stay away from that place."

Gorman's face had six more months of hell written on it.

Even Willis looked at me with a new furrow in his brow and I could see the fatal words for my performance report forming in his head: "Poor sense of timing. Has his own style. Not a team player."

He said, "Tomorrow morning, 8:00 sharp, the bulldozers start. There's going to be TV, newspapers there to catch the drama. Of which we want none. No Garnet Robson and no manure spreader or any other such tricks by him or anyone else. So, Tony, YOU take a cruiser out there, and YOU make sure nothing stops that digging."

North and east I drove to the quadrant of farms waiting for their morning rape. Behind the fence the old houses sagged, windows smashed like mouths with broken teeth. The mailboxes still waited for messages beside the road. I stopped for a minute in front of Garnet Robson's place and smelled the lilacs grown tall beside the porch. For the first time I wondered if I'd maybe taken a wrong turn, if I should have stuck it out a little longer as a typing teacher. Good holidays. Benefits. No old farmers to evict and persecute.

All night I drove the back road around the future dumpsite until the sun began to rise behind a gloom of clouds.

Seven-thirty in the morning, half an hour before official start time, I spotted the hole in the fence and stopped the car.

Clever. He'd picked a spot where the fence hid behind an outcrop of wild corn. For a minute I thought about just driving on.

Then a pair of headlights turned onto the concession road and I saw that it was another cruiser, Ted Gorman behind the wheel. Maybe coming to relieve me. Maybe just to make trouble. So I drove on, just lifted my hand like it's business as usual. When he'd turned the next corner I parked the cruiser deep down a laneway across from Robson's land.

It took longer than I expected to sprint back to the hole in the fence. I could hear Gorman's cruiser coming and ducked into the corn just in time. As he drove past, I caught a glimpse of a puzzled face, like he knew he ought to have met me again by now.

I struck into the field, running across rough furrows unturned for the last few seasons, through a stand of woodlot where I sank ankle deep into a bit of bog. Then through pasture and acres of old corn stubble, over fences, toward the barn brown and solid against the morning sky, wondering where I'd find him. In the barn, swinging from a beam? On the porch with a shotgun in his lap?

Then the chink of metal rang out of a stand of birches behind the barn. I ran toward it and stepped under the canopy of leaves.

Between the trees, Garnet Robson was digging. Bushel basket beside him, red buffalo check shirt on the ground, long-handled shovel in his hand, short handle on the ground. Digging.

There were only 10 minutes left till the bulldozers fired up. I thought, get him out of here, back the way you came. There was still time.

When he saw me he nodded, but the swing of his arms didn't falter.

He said, "I doubt there's anything left of it. But I had to see. And if there is, I got to take it away. It's only right."

Take what away? There was no breaking the fierce rhythm of those arms, so I grabbed the other shovel. Noises came from the other side of the barn, car doors slamming, the roar of machines warming up. I smelled Garnet's sweat, and my own, and something else, the flowers carpeting the ground beneath the birches. Odd little violets, elegant almost, with an extra round of petals and a sweet light scent mixed with the smell of fresh-turned earth. Like nothing I'd ever seen in my father's woods.

In the distance Gorman shouted, "The old coot's here someplace, and that kid's with him."

Garnet's shovel hit something hard. He dug carefully, lifting out small heaps of dirt until he'd uncovered with infinite gentleness a small metal box. An old tool box maybe, for old treasures? Coins? Papers?

Down on his knees he scraped away clay with his fingers, lifted out the box, but for all his care as it met the light the cover crumbled into dark flakes and we were looking down at bones.

A little skull. Bones of a tiny hand on folds of shredded fabric, earth stained but still recognizable: sailboats with red pennants flying on a blue striped breeze. Bones put into the ground 50 years ago, in the days when a country man took care of these things himself, and when fate miscarried he buried his sorrows and bore them in silence.

That was when Willis, Gorman, and a posse of reporters rounded the barn.

What I saw coming was crime scene tape, headlines, small bundle in a steel drawer, maybe even Garnet behind bars while the bureaucrats figured out that he was just an old man who needed to move some bones.

So, from his hands I took the box, set it down in the bushel basket. Covered it with the check shirt, threw in four quick shovels of earth. What next? It needed a layer of cover. Apples, pears, peaches, plums. None handy. But plants; my mother carted seedlings around her garden in a basket like this. So on top I spaded a clump of Jane Robson's Yorkshire violets. Then Garnet and I stepped out of the birches, each holding one handle of that basket.

Gorman grinned with pleasure and Willis opened his mouth to give me hell but before he said anything the young reporter from the *Courier* shouted, "Is Mr. Robson under arrest?"

"No, he is not." I said, to the snapping cameras. "Mr. Robson has been assisted in recovering a rare plant specimen. The excavation can start. Right on time."

I looked at Willis. He snatched, turned to the reporters and started herding them back toward the road. "Show's over. Digging starts in 15 minutes."

It helped that the next day's papers carried a picture of Garnet Robson, Sergeant Willis and the bushel basket, all under the headline: *Police Cooperation Saves Rare Species.*

It helped even more that the young reporter found the story of Jane Robson's violets so intriguing he wrote to England, and found those flowers had gone extinct in their native ground.

Two months later Garnet Robson was in Yorkshire bringing the violets back where they started, courtesy of the Botany Department, University of Durham, and I was posted ahead of schedule out of Port Rose.

Old Growth

In a little northern Ontario town called Chalk Narrows you'll find a municipal park on the bank of the Blackbird River. In the park stands a stone column, not much more than four feet high, and its bronze plaque tells you that it contains a time capsule. To be reopened in 100 years at a birthday party for a little lumber town that may not even exist by then.

I made that time capsule. Chalk Narrows was my second posting with the OPP, and I was a 27-year-old constable with amateur welding skills who got rooked into making the thing by a local politician. If my welding is good the papers stuck in there by school kids (newspaper clippings, fashion magazines, letters to the future, pages from a Canadian Tire catalogue) will be found intact by people who dress different, travel different, live different. But I doubt they'll be any different inside.

I sealed it up in October, 1997, just before Thanksgiving.

The same week that Blaise Conroy found me alone after hours long enough to tell me that he'd been carrying on with a married woman. And now a blackmailer had his hooks in the two of them. So many dollars, regular, or his head office and her husband would be told.

At 35 Blaise was a big man in his prime, tall, red haired. His large restless limbs and wide shoulders had the tight spring, caged in look of a man who'd been meant to work with his hands. It cost him a lot to say, "I need your help."

"It's not my job to judge you," I told Blaise. "You come to your own conclusions."

But I judged him and he knew it. What really made me mad was how he stood there looking tense, weary, and worried, but not one bit ashamed.

"I'm sorry for the turmoil it's caused," he said, his grey eyes meeting mine, his head high. "I never wanted to mess up her life. But I'm not sorry it happened. How can I be? It was the best thing that ever happened to me."

It might have bothered me less if it had happened at another time. If I'd been older, more experienced; if I hadn't just learned that my father had cancer. If I wasn't torn five ways in my own life and more confused than I'd ever been about what to do with myself.

As it was, it was a relief to rage at someone else.

In fact, I'd known about Blaise and some woman before he came to me with his blackmail problem. The week before, I'd seen them together in the woods. That was the same day my mother called and told me that a stubborn sore on my father's lip turned out to be malignant. There'd be surgery first, then radiation, then a waiting game to see if it came back. She was matter-of-fact about it like my family always is and I didn't say out loud that the news made my gut churn with fear and pity and loss. I was 2,000 kilometres from home and suddenly the distance seemed a sharp divide from everything old and familiar.

We're all different in the way we handle trouble. I've always needed the outdoors and a long walk to sort myself out. That's why I was there in the grove of pines when I saw a man and a woman embracing under the trees.

But I didn't think of going out to walk in the forest right away. The first thing I'd done with my mother's bad news was reach for the phone and Gail. Her warm voice had been sweet and sorrowful and full of love and she'd said, "It's the Lord's will, Tony. I'll pray for him. The Lord must be calling him home."

For a few hours I manned a speed trap thinking about Gail. About the first time I'd seen her in action; a hunter lost in the winter bush, how she, the town nurse practitioner, had gone out with the snowmobiles to find him with frozen feet. He still had those feet because of her. Gail with the soft blond hair and the relentlessly cheery look-on-the-bright-side smile, the Lord's will be done, and in a week and a half we were supposed to drive to Thunder Bay and Thanksgiving dinner to tell her parents that we were getting married.

A week and a half from now.

I delivered a summons and switched gears to thinking that you might know it's nonsense but you still think your parents will be there forever.

For the rest of that morning I sat at my desk shoving along the paperwork, including an application for a training course that would put me on promotion track. Which was where Gail wanted me to be; promotion track and regional HQ in Thunder Bay and a house down a street of bungalows from her Mom and Dad.

Then general orders came sliding out of the fax machine and Steve, the other constable, spent a few minutes spearing them to the bulletin board. Thunk, thunk went the thumbtacks and then a pause.

"Hey," he said, "Aren't you from this place? Eastern Ontario Division. Armagh Detachment."

"Yeah."

"They got an opening there."

He looked at me, eyebrows up, then passed the fax paper that had rolled itself into a diploma.

An opening in the Armagh Detachment. Armagh on the St. Lawrence north shore, the only place I'd ever called home. Where my brother farmed and my father might be dying.

Armagh was definitely not promotion track.

"Would you go back there?" asked Steve.

I didn't answer because that was when Jerome Skinner, Chalk Narrows' only shopkeeper and one of three school trustees, swung into the office saying, "Bob Forest tells me you know how to do a bit of welding."

I did. Growing up on a farm you learn to do a lot of things "a bit". My brother Mike had picked up the amateur vet skills. I had watched the local jack-of-all-trades with a torch long enough, been given enough scraps to fiddle with that I'd learned how to join two pieces of metal.

So I nodded, wondering what Jerome wanted.

If I was an amateur welder, Jerome Skinner was a recreational politician. He ran the grocery/hardware/video store where the whole town went to pick up the mail so he knew everyone and a lot about where their mail came from. We saw him daily, but like most politicians he smiled a lot and revealed little. I knew Jerome had been married and wasn't any more. That he spent a lot of time in the woods with binoculars and a bird book. That he got his picture in the regional paper a lot, so you knew he was a climber. It was always the same picture: Jerome in suit and tie wearing heavy-rimmed glasses and the polished apple look of a new graduate. It made him look a decade younger, taller and stronger than the skinny fellow who lifted and resettled those glasses as often as most people breathe.

"Hey, Jerome," said Steve, "By-election next month. I heard you were going for regional council next."

"That's right." Jerome said, then swung back to me, "Bob's got his arm in a sling. He was going to make the school a time capsule for the centennial cairn. Said you might be able to do it. You're welcome to use his equipment."

Jerome didn't wait for agreement, just unrolled a diagram of the stone column I'd seen going up in the Park. With it a pencil sketch of the bronze plaque it would wear:

This time capsule was placed by the Children of Van Horne Elementary School, October, 1997, to mark the 100th birthday of the town of Chalk Narrows. To be reopened at the bicentennial, 2097.

Then, in bigger letters, the names of the principal and trustees. I'd never seen Jerome's full handle before: Jerome Van Horne Skinner.

I was impressed. "You related to William Van Horne?" I asked. "Sir William Cornelius?"

"My mother's side." said Jerome briefly, like he was trying to be modest. William Van Horne is the kind of man who becomes a hero in a country that rarely goes to war. To earn his knighthood he'd built the CPR, and because he'd run the track through this chunk of the north his name was huge in the district. Van Horne Township. Sir William Van Horne Public Library. There was even a bar up in Dryden called Willie's.

"What are you putting into this time capsule?" I asked, mostly to stall for time. Did I want to make this thing? I didn't like Jerome's assumption that I would. On the other hand, our sergeant was big on community involvement.

"Stuff the school kids are gathering," he said, smiling like a man with a pet project. "It was my idea. The teachers say it's making them think about the world they live in now and how it might change. You know, fashions, how people make a living, world issues …"

What about the real questions, I thought morosely. What about death and loss and passion and death?

"How big you want this thing?"

"The cairn's four feet tall. A couple cubic feet, any shape would do."

"Alright," I said. "I'll go see Bob. I got a week for this, right?"

"Six days. We seal it up next Thursday."

•   •   •

Mid-afternoon I gave up pretending that the day you find out your dad has a terminal disease is an ordinary day. I drove the cruiser out along the river, thinking one more time that Chalk Narrows was one dog ugly town. Twelve-hundred people huddled on a riverbank in the middle of the bush a day's drive west and north of Thunder Bay. One grocery store/post office, one liquor store, a Sears outlet, one garage, one bar. Anything else you wanted was 100 kilometres north or south and there was nothing, not a gas station or a side road in either direction. My Southern Ontario notion that the acceptable distance between hamlets was roughly 15 kilometres had been shocked by all that space when I first arrived in the Narrows and settled in for a long winter.

Relationships were different in that isolation. If you wanted not to be lonely you learned to drink beer with a CPR brakeman, talk home construction with the priest. Maybe even find that you'd made a very evangelical woman your girlfriend. Very evangelical. Very much your girlfriend.

I parked the cruiser down the access road and walked into the old growth forest on the bank of the Blackbird River. I hadn't been posted to Chalk Narrows half a year before I discovered these woods. Ironically, it was Blaise Conroy who'd first walked me through Van Horne district's last unlumbered stand of pines.

"There's something about this place," he'd said, laying a freckled arm on the grey bark of a tree that had stood there for hundreds of years. "When I'm here I think there's a chance it might all make sense."

The Friday of that week before Thanksgiving I walked among the trees thinking they'd make fine straight timbers for a house. Then I thought about my father and my future and going home to Armagh and who might come with me. Or not.

Underfoot the pine needles made a soft carpet so thick no underbrush cluttered the stand of red and white pines. Sunlight sparkled on the river, but in the wind you could feel the cut of the coming winter. A hundred feet above my head the green tops swayed gently. The trees, so tall and straight, made a natural cathedral and, like every church I'd ever been in, failed on the issue of answers.

The trees creaked and a northern flicker called and I wondered how I'd ever get through another winter in this place and then I saw a man and a woman in the distance. As much for my own privacy as for theirs, I turned away.

But not soon enough.

The woman's back was to me, dark hair spilling over the freckled arm that circled her. The man leaned closer, as if to catch the tears suggested by that bent dark head. I turned to leave them alone but not before I saw without wanting to that the man was Blaise Conroy.

The Reverend Blaise Conroy if you please, Catholic priest, pastor of St. Joseph's Church, Chalk Narrows, Ontario. Father Conroy to half the town.

• • •

That night, as usual, I was out with Gail. It was routine, an evening of Chalk Narrows night life (options: bowling, drinking, hockey in winter, fishing and hunting in season, more drinking, more bowling), then a few hours at my place, then a late walk to the apartment she shared with the social worker.

We were in the Prince Hotel with a group of her friends, the social worker, a bush pilot, a clerk from the municipal office. It was a good group to hide in, thinking your own thoughts while they threw darts and laughed about the lamentable state of Canadian hockey. I was thinking about Blaise and a woman. Blaise, the priest and a promise to go it alone, and a woman likely to have made promises of her own.

Blaise. If you grew up Catholic the minute you heard the name you knew exactly how that guy had been raised. You knew his family got down on their knees and said the rosary every night before bed. That they ate fish on Fridays, went to Stations of the Cross in Lent and lined up for confession every first Friday of the month on a promise of plenary indulgence. You knew all that just from the name, because you yourself had been lined up along the altar rail every February 3rd, and the priest put your neck between two crossed candle sticks, asking St. Blaise who had saved a girl from choking on a fish bone to preserve you from a similar fate.

When I came to Chalk Narrows I met Blaise Conroy visiting the imprisoned (Tommy Dillon in the cells for drunk and disorderly). Right away, I pegged him as the good Catholic boy who'd bought the full program. Followed the approved trajectory from altar boy to seminary to dog collar. Whereas I, lesser mortal, had bailed out at the communion rail.

In another town I'd never have got to know the priest. But Chalk Narrows had a way of throwing people together. Blaise played hockey and was known to buy a round in the grubby lounge of The Prince Hotel. Over that beer I'd spent more than a few hours listening to him talk about the latest house his father was building back home in the Ottawa Valley. Post-and-beam construction. That was his dad's line of work and he'd get wistful and I'd get intrigued, looking at how differently a building went together when built of timbers and bents instead of two-by-four sticks. It wasn't long till copies of his dad's leftover plans wandered from Blaise's house to mine.

God only got into the conversation once, and even that happened over a set of plans. I'd said, "God, if my dad had a business like this instead of a dairy farm I could still be in beautiful sunny Southern Ontario."

I'd looked at him and laughed, stupidly, now that I think of it. "You must have got religion bad, eh, you being the only son. My dad would have had a fit if neither Mike or I had stayed on the farm. Silent fit, but we'd all know it. Bet your dad is seething."

But Blaise had shaken his head and his smile had been thin. "No. He's over the moon. Always wanted to be a priest himself."

• • •

"You're quiet tonight," said Gail when we got to my quarters.

I'd forgotten what a mess the place was. Brochures and drawings were strewn everywhere; kitchen table, coffee table, couch and floor, all papered with house plans.

They made me think again of Blaise, again of that woman leaning into his arms, but I still minded when Gail's hands swept the room, gathering the debris into tidy piles. I'd spent so many hours wondering if the gambrel roof or the saltbox or a steep pitch with dormers were more my thing. Wondering where I'd ever stay long enough to build it. Wondering if Mike might carve an acre lot out of his back forty for me.

"Leave it," I said, maybe a little too sharply because she looked up, surprised and came right to me.

"Worrying about your Dad?" A gentle hand rested on my arm. "I prayed for him all day. I have the strongest leading that he isn't going to die."

"We all die, Gail."

She looked shocked, even hurt, but tonight I had no patience for God. Or maybe it was his men that annoyed me.

"Of course we all die," she agreed, but her voice was soft with hurt. It was almost visible, the defences going up, the explanation cooking for how God could make death a good thing.

As if God were some cosmic tidying impulse like the one she obeyed, reducing my dream house to a square on the coffeetable. I pulled her down onto the couch and said, "Someday I'm going to build a house like that."

I didn't mention an acre in Armagh.

Gail had the softest skin, and my fingers ran up and down her white arm. I'd seen her hard-nosed and competent in her nursing clinic, on the phone with some doctor down the line who didn't think he couldn't admit a patient for surgery, and 10 minutes later she'd be loading a stretcher at the airstrip. For a long time it had been an appealing contrast: firm spine, soft heart, even softer body to draw towards me in the dark.

"I didn't see a bungalow in any of those brochures," she said, dubiously.

"So I'll design you one. A two-storey bungalow. Steep roof pitch. Huge windows."

"Silly. A bungalow only has one-storey."

"There's nothing religious about a bungalow is there?"

Mistake. Gail didn't like to be teased about God. It wasn't until we'd crossed the big hurdles that I'd discovered the full scope of God's involvement in Gail's life. (How He'd led her to pick Chalk Narrows for her first full time job; how He'd helped land a Cessna on a choppy lake so she could bring a boy with third-degree burns to Winnipeg.) I'd even had to give a few seconds consideration to her idea that we'd been brought together as part of a celestial plot for human happiness. Partly intrigued and partly annoyed at the idea of a huge Someone mucking into what I thought was my business.

For a nanosecond, I thought of telling Gail about the priest and a woman in the old growth forest. Though Gail belonged to another branch of the God business, I knew she'd feel as I did. Knew she'd condemn, knew she's have chapter and verse at the ready, and for some reason that made me feel worse, not better. So I turned to her for other comfort.

Hours later I pulled the covers around us and tried one more time to get her to stay the night.

"It wouldn't be right," she said.

"I don't get it. Where the hell's that written: 'Thou shalt not wake up together'?"

"Tony!"

"Well, I really don't get it. Sex is ok; breakfast isn't."

She sat up, reached for her clothes and explained it patiently, like she was dumbing down a complex concept for a little kid. "It's okay because we're getting married."

"But we …" Something vulnerable in her face stopped me. Gail had strong ideas about these things, but I didn't think we'd exactly followed the approved order, no matter what she was telling herself.

• • •

I avoided Blaise for days. Didn't see Gail much either because our shifts didn't match. In my spare time I fiddled with Jerome's centennial project and brooded on human frailty and a posting in Armagh.

Blaise found me in Bob's shop trying to turn a piece of four-inch steel column from a truck drive shaft into a time capsule. Then he told me that he and Anna Foster had been carrying on for the best part of a year. That they'd decided it had to end, for the sake of her kids and his old dad whose heart would break over a fallen priest for a son. And that he was being blackmailed by Jerome Skinner. And, no, he wasn't sorry.

Fooling around with another man's wife. Blackmailed for thousands of dollars. And he wasn't sorry.

I'd had four days to think about Blaise having an affair. Now I had to wrap my mind around the idea of Anna, Anna Foster and Charlie. Charlie Foster who worked for the CPR, played defence when he wasn't on the railroad, a Labatt's man.

And Anna. In the tumble of thoughts I recognized one with surprise: that Anna Foster was a woman a man could love.

I knew Anna Foster from the little volunteer library. Not many people in Chalk Narrows wanted to talk about books and over the counter she'd sparkled with suggestions, sometimes taken mine, and I'd made a point of visiting the library when Anna was on duty. She had long dark hair and a sprinkle of freckles across her nose, always a smile but always a focus in the blue eyes like she was thinking, thinking, living inside her head.

"Try this," she'd say, passing me a book she'd loved, "The mystery gets a little thin in the middle but a great blend of history. I felt like I'd been to rural Maine." Or New South Wales. Or St. Petersburg. Or England, said Anna who never went anywhere.

"What about Charlie?" I asked Blaise.

Morality isn't part of a constable's job description, but I still wanted to deck him on behalf of a decent guy who worked hard for his wife and family and just didn't deserve this.

Blaise didn't waver. "They married when she was 18. Did their best but it wasn't a real choice for either of them."

"They've got kids. Four, if I remember right."

"Don't talk to me like that, Tony. I remember the number. I remember their names too, Sarah, Melanie, Meghan, and Patrick."

He unfolded arms held tight across a broad chest and glared at me, one of the few men in town tall enough to meet me at eye level. "Why do you think we've decided it's got to end? Do you think we love each other one bit less? Not one damn bit less. But we're thinking about all of them, all the others, the kids, Charlie, my parents. So don't talk to me like that."

"Charlie doesn't know?"

"No, thank God, Charlie doesn't know."

"So you paid Skinner and he kept quiet. What do you want from me?"

His smile was cheerless, as if he recognized that I still wasn't going to make this easy for him. Maybe even caught a glimmer of the fact that this was how people with their heads screwed on right would always react.

"I'm here because he hasn't stopped. Of course he hasn't stopped. Threatened to go to the bishop." Blaise smiled, a bleak grimace of defeat. "But at least there I'd got in ahead of him. Of course I'm being moved. His excellency wants me at the Lakehead by Thursday."

In two days, he'd be gone. "So you move on with your nice life. Anna stays behind in this town with that creep looking at her for the next 40 years."

"I won't go if it's left like that. He's got to be shut up. I can't leave her with that."

"I could arrest him right now."

"You're not making this easy, are you, Tony? You know as well as I do that would be just as bad. It would all come out. Charlie would know. The whole town would know. If you're thinking of those kids you've got to help us."

I didn't like it, but he was right. The book said a blackmailer needed to be arrested, let the pieces fall where they may. Something else said silence was the better choice. I thought about it. It wasn't procedure. It wouldn't fly past Steve, who, by luck of the unworthy, happened to be in Kenora that day. If anyone found out about this it wouldn't look like an attempt to save a marriage, it would look, especially with a priest in the mix, like a cover-up.

"How do you suggest I do this?"

"Talk to him. Shake him up. You're the cop. Let him know you're watching and if he slips up he's in for it."

I thought about it. Then a heavier weight seemed to settle on Blaise, a grimmer despair in the lines around his eyes.

"One more thing," he said. "Jerome would never have made a move, no matter what he thought was going on, without evidence."

I sighed. "What's he got?"

• • •

That was Tuesday night. In two days I would drive Blaise to Dryden to catch a flight for the Lakehead, but wouldn't leave town if things were not fixed with Jerome Skinner.

In between was Wednesday. Not much time to retrieve the evidence, silence Jerome, finish a time capsule in time for the Thursday ceremony and, maybe, keep a family together.

Over breakfast, between distracting glances at timber frame and post-and-beam drawings, I wondered how I could deal with Jerome in any way that didn't involve brute force. He was smaller and older, and yes, I could look scary if I wanted to. But did I want to? Would it be effective? He could make any promise while looking at a fist but that would wear off. And then there were those letters.

For consolation I took a bundle of plans to work with me. It'd be a relief to have something to look at under lunch.

All morning I thought about the knot Blaise had tied and now expected me to untangle. Lovers must be fools to leave so many traces. Blaise said they'd left a bundle of letters all in one place because Anna's house wasn't safe and the parish had provided him with a housekeeper known for weekly mattress turning. An abandoned cabin downriver had become their meeting place, and their mailbox.

"Even when she wasn't there I felt like I was with her," he'd said. And then stopped because he could see I didn't want to hear any of that.

But they hadn't counted on Jerome. Those high-powered bird watcher binoculars had spied more than feathers one day in the woods, and then he'd watched and waited until he found the cabin, and the letters.

I couldn't turn Jerome upside down and shake them out of his pockets. I needed something, some leverage. Something he wanted in return?

His time capsule would be done tonight. Worth a trade? Tell him he'd look a fool when no metal cylinder turned up?

Not good enough.

I still had no solution, no strategy either, when I went to the Prince for lunch and Rosie, my favourite waitress, took my order.

"BLT on brown," I said, "and a coffee."

All 200 fun and foul-mouthed pounds of Rosie were Irish. She'd be about 40 but looked older, likely from the cigarette always dangling from her mouth.

"You know, Rosie," I said, "My Dad always has a roll-your-own hanging right there from the same corner. Every day, every minute I can remember. MacDonald's Export in the tin. Keeps it on the tractor with a package of papers."

"Where's this tale goin', lad?" Her eyes narrowed and it was clear she was sick of being told. But I forged on.

"Well, my mom called the other day. He's got cancer."

"And you're sharing this wondrous news because...?"

"Because I like you, Rosie."

She slapped me on the head affectionately with her order pad and shuffled off to the kitchen. I unrolled my plans and was disappointed to find I'd brought the wrong ones — not the timber frame young man's dream. I'd brought the papers for the cairn and the plaque to go in the park.

When Rosie reappeared and dropped the cup and saucer on top the cigarette was gone.

"Don't be getting a bloody saviour complex," she glared. "T'was the fag end anyway." Then her expression changed, "But I'm sorry to hear about your Da."

"Thanks, Rosie."

"What's this, then?" she asked, looking at the plans, "You think we need tablecloths in the Prince?"

"Brought the wrong ones actually. Jerome wants me to make a time capsule for this thing they're putting up in the park.."

"Jerome, is it?" Rosie's mouth shrank and pursed and she looked at the papers like she'd stub a cigarette there if she'd only had one handy. "What's himself up to now, the pompous ass?" Her eye caught the diagram of the plaque. "Oh, of course he'd want the name there. The name must be read by all."

She leaned close to read it and then laughed quietly. "The lying bugger."

"What's that, Rosie?"

She punched a nicotine stained finger on the name of trustee Jerome Van Horne Skinner. "The biggest suck up in the western world, is Jerome." Except she pronounced it sook up. "The bastard's middle name is Francis. He's no more Van Horne than I'm Princess Di."

"How do you know that, Rosie?"

"I was married to the bugger, wasn't I? He's likely forgotten the inconvenient fact, like he's forgotten his middle name. Or the arrogant bastard thinks I never knew. I'll get your lunch," she said, and headed off to the kitchen, still chuckling.

So, along with bacon, lettuce and tomato, Rosie had served up some leverage. I ate my sandwich thoughtfully, then went back to the detachment and conducted a search of motor vehicle registrations. Sure enough, there was the blue Buick with the vanity plate (AIM4KPS) registered in the name of Jerome Francis Skinner.

Leverage. But was it enough?

• • •

That evening I paid Jerome a visit as the store was closing.

"Have a word?" I said to him, with the plans for the centennial cairn rolled under my arm.

He snapped the locks behind the last customer, looking peeved. "This about the time capsule? You're going to make the deadline, aren't you?"

"Sure." I said, "I've got the thing ready to close."

"Great." He looked puzzled. "So what do you want?"

"You got that bronze plaque made up?"

"I do," he said, "As a matter of fact they attached it to the cairn today. It's already down there in the park."

"That's too bad," I said. "There's an error in it."

He resettled the glasses, looking at me carefully.

"What's that?"

"Your name, Jerome. It's not right."

"Spelled wrong?"

"No. The wrong name. It's not Van Horne is it?"

"How would you know?"

"I do know. That's enough. And you wouldn't want anyone else to find out you'd been gilding the lily would you?"

His face thinned, the eyes behind the glasses narrowed and glittered.

"Gilding the lily," I said, "That's a Shakespearean phrase, but of course you know that. It's the kind of thing politicians like to do."

"What do you want?"

I ignored him. "It's like claiming a degree you never earned, military service no one can find records for. The kind of thing that really helps a career. Especially at election time. You are planning a run for council aren't you?"

"You shut up." The face behind the dark frames was white.

"Nice step up from school board that would be. Mayor the next time around. After that, who knows? You joined a federal party yet? I'd say your chances up here favour the …"

"What is it you want?" he yelled.

"I want a package of letters you found in a cabin downriver. There's 27 of them. I want them all."

He looked almost relieved.

"So I give you the letters. Then what?"

"Then I don't arrest you for blackmail. Don't tell everyone in the town your real name. Francis. That's kind of a sissy name, isn't it? No wonder you don't want it on the plaque."

For a minute he tried to look cocky. "Why do you care about that crooked cheat? They're all like that, those priests, cassock and lace doily robes. 'Yes, Father. No, Father. Of course, Father.' The biggest hypocrites and liars to walk the earth."

He looked ready to spit and I knew that whatever Jerome had against Blaise, it had nothing to do with him running around with Anna; everything to do with the Roman collar he wore.

I let him mull it over. Then I said, "You've had your run. He's headed out of town. You get your posh name fresh and shiny on that plaque and everyone moves on with life. Unless you make a slip. I'll be transferred out of here soon, but when I go Anna Foster will know all about the gilded lily."

He settled those glasses one more time. Stared at me with lips thin as wire. Finally led the way to the back of the store, stepped into an office piled high with storage cartons. Unlocked a desk drawer, reached far into the back and pulled out a bundle of papers, tied with a white ribbon.

"Isn't that sweet," he sneered, and tossed the bundle to me.

•   •   •

I locked the letters in the car, finished the time capsule just before midnight and woke up the next morning to a call from the principal saying the ceremony had been postponed a day because of the rain.

So I drove Blaise to Dryden with the windshield wipers going hard all the way and neither of us said a word. He knew what I thought and he wasn't going to lower his head. I stared ahead at the wet highway. He looked out the window with a face as bleak as the northern stones.

At the airport I said, "What should I do with the letters?"

"Burn them."

Then he thanked me for helping and walked off through the driving rain with a single bag in his hand, and even then he held his head high.

It was dark by the time I got home. I took the letters out of the glove compartment, went inside, made a sandwich, and then I made a mistake.

I read the letters.

Why? Pure, impure curiosity. How had they started? How had they managed so long in a town so small? What had they felt and how had they said what they felt?

I wanted to read them and finding a justification wasn't hard. Perhaps Jerome had read them. No perhaps, he most certainly had, and wouldn't it make sense to know what was in them so I'd know if he was using any part of these words to bother Anna?

So I gave the white ribbon a few tugs and then I began to read.

Ten minutes in the phone rang and I lifted my head from another world, almost thought of not answering. But I did, and it was Gail, on her break at the clinic.

"Hi, honey," she said, "I'm back on day shift tomorrow so we can head out for my parents' in good time. Think we'll be there by nine or ten?"

It took a few seconds to realize what she meant. Thanksgiving weekend. Her parents. The big announcement.

"Yeah. Right."

"You okay? Still worrying about your dad?"

"I'm al — "

"Hey, I heard the priest got sent out of town. Left this morning."

"I drove him, Gail."

"Really? So what's the story? Dipping into the treasury?"

I didn't answer but it didn't seem to matter.

"Not worse, I hope. My God, I hope he wasn't one who liked the boys? Was he?"

My eye landed on an open page with a handwritten poem and the page rested on a sketch of the elegant Kingpost truss, my favourite.

"None of the above. And I can't talk about it."

"Oh."

When I hung up and went back to the letters it felt like stepping back into the woods, into a world that was green and old and ran roots deep into good ground.

One envelope after another, bent at the corners, some a little water stained. When I was done I knew they shouldn't burn. They were just words, just the story of something wrong, misplaced, out of bounds. But they were also fine and beautiful and what would it hurt if a hundred years from now when Blaise and Anna were dust, what would it hurt if someone found these letters and saw that something fine?

So I drove over to Bob's shop, borrowed his cutoff saw, sliced off the top of the time capsule, and into a roll of newspaper clippings, fashion magazines, handwritten notes and cute pictures from the kindergarten class I stuffed a set of 27 letters. Grabbed a hunk of insulation out of the wall and stuffed it on top. At 3,300 degrees Celcius the metal melted and joined again and there was the Chalk Narrows time capsule, good for a hundred years. With a small surprise for the future, for the part of us that doesn't change no matter what coin we spend or what we wear or how we travel.

Then I got in the car and drove fast down the one road, south toward the border, punched a Chieftains CD into the deck and turned it up loud.

Gail hated this music.

Track 12, full volume, "The Wind That Shakes the Barley". Two minutes and fifty seconds of tin whistle yelling that you only have the one life. Pipes and fiddles demanding attention to the warning in those letters: "If you and I were all …"

I wanted to feel that if; the longing and the knowing. The bohran banged no surrender. "If this were the only hour and the last place." I knew I'd never felt that, not yet. Never yet. And I didn't want to die without having been there.

I hit track 12 over and over again, the wind swept the barley for a hundred kilometres of pipes, fiddles and drums and by the time I turned back to Chalk Narrows I knew two things.

I wanted that posting in Armagh.

And I wouldn't be going to Thunder Bay for Thanksgiving.

A Red River Cruise

We searched for Sietse Fennema's body for six long hours. At the edge of an ice-crusted field I stepped into the woods and stood listening. Frozen fingers cracked above my head on the breath of a wind and ice shards fell into my hair, trickling in shivers down the collar of my coat.

Out on the field, moving forward in a slow grid, the volunteer firemen and members of the Dutch Reformed Church advanced step by step, searching for any sign of the old Dutch farmer, missing since the end of the storm. For 10 days, while a rain of ice downed power lines and crumpled barns, our Eastern Ontario backroads had huddled in the cold and dark. It didn't take much imagination to know that if we found Sietse Fennema, we'd find him dead.

Stepping back out onto the field, I shouted a warning, "Don't get under the trees!"

One strong wind and the fingers of ice suspending broken trunks 30, 40 feet above us would come crashing down. I wasn't about to sacrifice the living to find a corpse likely already stripped by storm starved wolves.

Under the slate February clouds we moved forward slowly, 10 feet apart. My legs ached from constant sliding on uneven furrows. My eyes scanned left to right, searching for any sign that the old farmer had wandered this way in the storm. Once, eyes racing to a flash of red, I spotted a young cardinal frozen under the glass.

"Hey! Over here!" a voice bellowed from the far side of the field.

We tramped eagerly to the fenceline where a fireman pointed to a tobacco pouch frozen on a stack of unused posts, embedded in the ice like an insect caught in amber.

The missing man's son, Sam Fennema, edged to the front of the group and looked down with us. He stood silent, unblinking eyes and wide mouth revealing nothing. All his windburnt face told was that he'd been out in the cold for a long time.

I said, "I don't think it means anything. It's too far under the ice. That pouch was there when the rain started. Mr. Fennema went missing after it stopped."

Only then did Sam speak. "Yeah. That makes sense. I stopped here when I was plowing last fall. It's probably been here since then."

We didn't go back to the search right away. Cigarette packs came out, matches flared and fell to a hissing death on the ice. The men were tired, cold, and discouraged. We'd been tramping the fields for hours and had one pointless tobacco pouch to show for it.

"We'll finish this field and call it a day, guys." I announced.

"Hold on!" Young Fennema's head jerked up, "You can't quit! There's an hour of light left. We've only done the closest fields."

"I know. But it'll take a while to walk back."

"We have to find him." Sam Fennema insisted, glaring at me with more anger than anxiety.

Calling off a search is a tough thing. Old Bill at the police college used to rank it with delivering news of fatalities and other thankless duties. But the time to quit always comes, and someone has to say it has.

The men reformed the line across the field and left me, the policeman, to handle Sam. They would have spoken up if they wanted to continue. I knew I couldn't have stopped them from looking all night if there were any hope of finding the old man alive. But they didn't want to be the one to tell their neighbour it wasn't worth the danger to find his father's bones.

"This was a long shot," I reminded him. "It doesn't mean he was out here, or is out here. It just means we didn't find anything today. We can try again tomorrow."

"Not tomorrow." he said. "Not on Sunday. So we should look now, longer. We could get another field done in an hour."

"These guys can't afford to break a leg, sliding around in the dark. They have their own farms to keep going. We're quitting after this field, and we'll be back tomorrow."

"Not tomorrow. My father would never want that. Not on Sunday." I'd forgotten how strict some Dutch Reformed churches were about Sunday observance. At that moment, cold and frustrated, I'd had enough.

"Then you call all these volunteers back at your convenience," I snapped, and turned to slide back across the ice.

"That's not what I mean and you know it," he yelled at my back.

•   •   •

Standing under the hot shower spray, I was just as stung by the way the day ended. After we found nothing in the last field we'd trudged back to Fennema's farmyard. In the gathering dark no one said much, just stood near their cars, reluctant to go. It was a silent thing, the way their support passed to Sam in the huddling dark, man to man, farmer to farmer, old to young.

Sam shook hands with each man as he left. "Thanks for coming out. Thanks for helping. Thanks for giving up the day. 'preciate it."

Except for me. Not a word.

Skin tingling in the hard spray, I thought back to how Sam Fennema showed up in our OPP detachment five days ago. I'd looked up, glad to be distracted from the stack of reports on my desk. Sam had stood in his big parka, well away from the counter, eyes adjusting from the winter glare while he looked at the safety posters and fake plants like a man who never expected to find himself visiting the police.

I was glad to see him, or anyone who'd break the tedium. After the excitement of the storm it was harder than ever to maintain a conscientious interest in paperwork.

Sam tapped the slush off his boots, stepped up to the counter and said, "My father is missing. Since the storm."

"What's your father's name?" I reached for an incident report and a pen.

"Fennema. Sietse Fennema." He spelled it, each letter surrounded by a silence that defied comment on the old Frisian name.

"And you are?"

"Sam Fennema."

"Tony Aardehuis," I introduced myself. "You're from Kerry Townshop, eh? I grew up out there."

For the first time the pale blue eyes registered more than my uniform. He looked at my dirty blond hair and the trademark Aardehuis nose and a light of recognition flared. "You related to the guy with the Guernsey herd?"

"That's my brother Mike."

The tense lines around his wide mouth relaxed. Rapport established, I pushed on.

"So, how long has your father been missing, Sam?"

"Nine days. I know it's a long time. But I thought he'd gone to someone's house during the storm. He lives across the road from the farm. Has his own little house."

I knew the pattern: a farmer's son like me, he'd stepped into the acres like my brother Mike, and the parents moved into a retirement bungalow on land severed from the farm.

"One day, second week of the storm he was just gone. We've been cut off since then, road closed, no phone, so I couldn't report it."

"How old is he?"

"Seventy-seven."

"Did he have heat during the storm?"

"Woodstove, same as us."

"Why didn't he move in with you during the storm? You know, to save fuel."

"He wouldn't come."

I couldn't tell if Sam's brittle replies were his natural style. Or if finding himself at the police station froze a naturally warmer man. But even that first day I heard no wail of desperate worry in his voice.

Odd too, that his elderly father suffered through those grim weeks alone. Not a day of it passed before Mike moved my own parents into the farm house where he knew they'd be warm, and where my father's old bones could take no spills struggling back and forth to the woodpile. Sure, there were tensions, three generations under one roof with no lights or TV. But Mike would never have left them on their own.

"Why wouldn't he come?"

"He didn't want to."

"Why?"

His lips pursed in a prudish frown. My father always said the Frisians were the most private people.

But I waited. Old Bill always said that silence more than anything loosens the tongue.

Even the tongue of a Frisian farmer. Reluctantly, Sam said, "We had a disagreement. Just before the storm hit."

"About?"

"I wanted to enlarge the herd. Build a new barn."

He stopped. I leaned conversationally across the counter. "And?"

"And that's all. But he wouldn't come near the house. My wife made him supper, sent it over with the kids. Then he was gone."

"Maybe the army brought him in to the emergency shelter?"

He shrugged. "Could have."

"You check?"

He shrugged again. "No time. We've had so much damage from the storm …"

It was the shrug that reminded me of a story told after the Manitoba flood. A tall tale maybe, passed from cop to cop, and I never knew if it was true. Or just another myth written in the adrenalin rush of disaster.

They say this old lady was found floating down the Red River in a rowboat. Sitting up straight in her wheelchair, dead long enough to keep that shape when they lifted her out. No one ever reported her missing or claimed the body, though she looked well cared for. Hand knit sweater. Home perm. Good dentures.

It seemed like someone just got tired of cleaning those teeth and took the chance provided by nature and a swollen river.

Goodbye, granny. Off you go, on the trip of a lifetime.

• • •

When I told him we had a missing person, the sergeant said, "That the Sam Fennema who used to pitch for the county team?"

I nodded.

"Guy had a great arm. We'd have made the provincials, but he wouldn't take the time off the farm anymore."

"He's a good farmer. Steady winner at the Royal Winter Fair."

"You would know, eh? Dutch boy, Kerry Township, must be near your age. You go to school with him?"

"No. He went to that Christian school."

The sergeant's pencil drummed on the desk. All week he'd been stuck there, chained to the grindstone of post-storm reports. The region, looking for a fat relief cheque from the federal government, wanted documentation of every move we'd made during the crisis.

"Any family the old guy might have gone to?"

"Sam's an only child. No other relatives in Canada."

"Poor old fella's probably frozen to death on the back forty. But maybe he buggered off somewhere. You never know." He looked at the papers, looked at the chance to get off the hook, and sighed.

"Drive out there and see if he turned up at the shelter."

• • •

I took the cruiser out to Kerry, travelling in a glare of sunshine on a sea of frozen glass. Along the highway, snapped telephone poles lay in the ditches like casualties of war. I tried not to look beyond them at the trees tortured by the weight of ice into unnatural bows of submission. Or think of the decades that would have to pass before the maples and oaks, tall and regal, regained their pride.

"The storm of the century", the papers called it. A rain of ice that plunged us for two weeks in the heart of an Ontario winter into cold and dark. Live wires littered the road, buildings collapsed, cattle died of cold or electrocution.

And through it all I'd remembered old Bill saying: "Crime's doorway is distraction."

What could be more distracting than 233 square kilometres with the lights out, phone lines down and all eyes firmly fixed on a dwindling supply of firewood and lamp oil?

Not that we had any crime. We came out of the storm like winners of the Norman Rockwell Good Neighbours Award. We'd sheltered, fed and cut wood for each other, and come through the disaster with not one casualty.

Until Sam Fennema walked into the detachment.

• • •

My first stop, I talked to Alison Bruce, a nurse from the County General who'd set up and run an emergency shelter in the grade school. At the height of the storm 500 people slept there on gym mats and Alison fed and blanketed them all.

I found her in front of her house, clearing broken branches from the driveway. When I explained what I wanted, she pitched a last stick onto the pile and said, "Thank God for an excuse to quit."

While coffee dripped in a brown stream into the carafe, Alison leaned comfortably against the kitchen counter and said, "Look at the lovely steam rising. It's such a wonder to have electricity again."

"You don't miss all the excitement, then?"

"Lord, no!" She scanned my clean-shaven face, the pressed uniform pants. "Tell me you didn't appreciate pulling that shirt out of the drier this morning." I felt like a kid, kindly patted on the head. Five grades ahead of me through school, Alison has always been able to put me in my place.

The log book from the shelter was just as orderly. It said that Sietse Fennema had indeed turned up there, brought in by the army, stayed four days, and left again.

"Where did he go?"

"I don't know."

"You didn't keep track?"

"He's a grown man, Tony, not a kid signing out of school."

I sipped Alison's good strong coffee standing in the sparkling cleanliness of her tidy kitchen. "What was the old guy like, Alison? You know, was he with it? Did he maybe just wander off?"

"Stop calling him old. He was sharp as a tack. Beat the young guys at cards every day. The only funny thing about him was the way he kept switching languages in the middle of a sentence."

"My parents do that too," I sighed. "More every year."

• • •

The ancestral home was only three miles out of the village and it was lunch time, so I dropped in on my parents.

It was odd, that reversion to the old language as the roots in Canada grew deeper. Half the kids in my school came from Dutch immigrant families, but every one of us walked into Grade One speaking English. Even if our parents barely could. They gave us pronounceable first names, which is why Sam Fennema isn't Sietse like his father and I'm not Teunis like mine. But as they aged the language they had learned first reclaimed its dominance.

Over a lunch of rye bread and smoked horse meat sliced thinner than paper I tried to decipher my father's assessment of Sietse Fennema.

"*Een echte ouwe taaie.*"

A real old tough? A hard bread?

"English, Dad. Something I can put in my report."

"*Stijf.* He was always stiff. *Een goede* farmer. Good met de land but tight met de money. You never heard dat he spent een cent on de house. Shust on de barn."

"*Hard voor de* wife." my mother interrupted.

"Ja, well. *Gereformeerd.*" Dad's hard hand waved dismissively over the coffee cups, explaining it all. "*Zwarte kousen.*"

Black stockings. What he meant was that the Fennema clan belonged to the strictest variety of Dutch Reformed Calvinists. Their old women wore black to church, their children went to Christian schools, and they clung to the belief that us wild living Catholics were bound for the flames. Or so my father said.

After lunch I stopped in the barn for a long breath of the smell of my childhood: dusty hay, dry grain, warm milk in the cat's bowl. All this could have been mine, but I'd thrown it over for my career of action and adventure writing seat belt citations for the OPP.

I found my brother Mike communing with a pen of feeding heifers.

"You know anything about those Fennemas? Have a place on Robson Road?"

Mike considered for a minute. Said he just knew them from around. Sietse he only knew as a scrawny, fierce looking old man. But Sam Fennema was a good guy. Uptight, but he worked hard.

"He came by last summer, looking at the milking parlour. Thought he'd update his if he could buy more quota and expand his herd."

"Say anything about his father?"

"Old Sietse? Sam didn't say much. But I got the idea he was looking for ways to convince the old man."

Mike's arm ran gently down the curve of a tan and white belly and I saw that the heifer was pregnant.

"Did he need the old man's cooperation to make the changes?"

"Didn't say. If it was a buyout, like I have with Dad, he might have had to wait for a payment." Mike looked up suddenly from beside the cow. "What's with all the questions?"

"Old Fennema disappeared. During the storm."

"No kidding." Mike stood still, pondering. "Out in the fields?"

"Could be. But he was in town at the shelter awhile."

"Maybe he took off for some place warm."

"Ha, ha. A Friese boer in Miami."

"That's cute when you talk Dutch," said my big brother, and shook his head, "I bet you think Sam bumped him off to get the farm. Grow up, Tony."

·   ·   ·

The sergeant said, "It's all yours. Have a look at the old guy's place. Talk to the army. Maybe they saw something when they went up and down there. Talk to Highways, find out when that road was opened."

Right off the bat I found that Sam Fennema had driven into town behind the sander three days before he bothered to report his father missing, so I drove out to Sam's farm for a chat.

The rough gravel of Robson Road connected the provincial highway and a regional road but it wasn't a detour anyone took for the sake of convenience. The isolated farm followed the same pattern as Aardehuis acres: grey barn, solid farmhouse, retirement bungalow, responsible son.

Sam faced me in the chill living room of his father's empty house and said, "Yeah, ok, I had to get supplies. I was thinking he'd gone to stay with someone he knew. Maybe someone from the church."

"Did you ask around?"

"No. I was too embarrassed."

"Why?"

"Because he should have been here! He might as well go around with a billboard saying he had a rotten son."

"Well he didn't do that. He went to the shelter and had a fine old time telling stories and playing cards."

"Cards?" His face tightened, lips pinched. "Cards?"

"What's the problem?"

"The kerk frowns on gambling."

"He was just playing cards."

"All the same."

Sam went back to his barn and I stayed, poking around the little house, trying to get a feel for the old man who had disappeared. I could hear Alison snapping, "Stop calling him old."

But it was hard not to. At 77 what could Sietse Fennema be, but old? The old guy. The old man. The old fella.

The old fella's walls hung with orderly rows of blue and white Delft. A black Bible with leather binding and gold edges lay on an end table. Oak immigrant furniture lined up symmetrically with the fake fireplace in the middle.

I looked at the family portrait. Sam, who clearly took after his mother, was just a kid in that picture. Mrs. Fennema, a well-padded, buxom woman looked like she should be presiding over cups of hot dark coffee, passing plates of almond cake and spice cookies. But Sietse stood with his chin jutting up, the sinews of his skinny neck taut above the collar of a Sunday suit. Under a single heavy eyebrow his eyes stared, intent, at the camera and a crooked smile twisted up one end of his mouth.

It was an empty, abandoned room. I took pity on the silent clock, pulled up the dangling brass weights, adjusted the time and gave the pendulum a push. While I waited to see if it was running right, I looked into the hand painted scene on the clock face.

Behind the moving hands lay a world of thatched farms on grey canals under trees forever bending to the wind. In the distance the sails of a windmill turned.

I was 27. At t27 Sietse Fennema had picked up everything he owned, left those canals, thatched roofs and turning sails and crossed an ocean to begin again. Then he'd ended up here, alone in a small house where he listened to the clock tick and watched his son begin to decide for himself where the straight lines should fall.

• • •

When I finally traced Corporal Armand Pelletier who'd driven down Robson Road that third week of January, he told me on the telephone that they'd checked on the residents of the Fennema farm twice. The first time, Sietse had refused to come to town.

"Did he look scared?" I asked.

"They was all looking scared then."

But he confirmed that the missing man had come in to the shelter with him on their second pass two days later. Corporal Pelletier knocked on Sam's farmhouse door, got no answer. Then the old man waved at him from across the road.

Even the corporal called him the old man. The old man said everyone was in the barn, and he wanted to get in to town.

In the background a radio blared, metal clanged, a voice shouted to keep it down. Information lay in hiding here, if only I asked the right questions.

"Did he say why he changed his mind about going to the shelter?"

"Can't remember, really. He looked 'appy to me. More than the first time we pass. Like he was going on holiday or something. *Vraiment* ... he was 'appy to be going to that shelter."

"Like he was getting away?"

He didn't understand. "Well, they was that way, eh? Cold, hungry. You blame them? There was no heat for two weeks."

"Did you bring him back to the farm some days later?"

"Not me."

"Did he say anything at all about his son?"

"No," the corporal said.

Instinct told me to wait for more.

"But I thought it was strange that he did not want to say goodbye to his people. Said he's left a note on the kitchen table. But there was no note in that kitchen. None that I saw."

• • •

The soft-spoken Dutch Reformed minister checked around his congregation and reported that no one had seen Sietse Fennema during or after the ice. He said the Fennemas had always been upstanding members of the church and examples of good Christian living. All of them. You couldn't find a better father or a kinder son.

Then he ran out of praises and said something useful.

"If Mister Fennema were to get upset, or lose his bearings so to speak, I'm not saying he did, you know, but if it were to happen so and so ..."

"Yes?"

He took a deep breath. "I've noticed many of the older congregants take a trip back to Holland during times of particular stress."

A far-fetched thought. A 77-year-old farmer with no suitcase, no money, unable to complete a sentence in a single language, gets out of the storm zone to an operational airport where he purchases a ticket to the Netherlands. But it was the only idea going, so I called Immigration and all the airlines carrying European flights out of Toronto and Montreal.

Sietse Fennema had not passed their way.

Still, I asked Sam to come in to the detachment and call his uncle in Holland.

My dad always said that Frisian is its own language. After listening on the other line I knew it was true, but I didn't need a translator to tell me Sam had been given a tongue-lashing.

He put down the receiver with a thump, a deep blush of humiliation creeping up the broad face. "He hasn't seen or heard from him."

For the first time, I felt sorry for Sam. He'd lived in a box all his life. Respect your elders. Family business stays in the family. Faith. Order. A good farmer is a good man. But when he pushed hard on that side of the box the whole thing tipped over.

Then Sam asked, "If we can't find him, what am I going to do? Do I make payments into his bank account even if he isn't here? If he's dead and we never find him, how does the farm get transferred?"

I didn't feel sorry for him anymore. "Find a lawyer." I said.

That was when I stopped playing around and began to believe that Sam Fennema had murdered his father. He had the motive: with his father out of the way he'd be the owner of a fine farm, no strings attached. If he'd lied to me about picking his father up at the shelter he'd had the opportunity. The storm of the century had provided the means.

Maybe he hadn't planned to do it, maybe it had just come out of the moment. Just one more argument about the future of the farm on the way back from town and Sam says: "Okay. You don't like it, get out and walk."

And the old man, left beside the road, falls and dies, and Sam comes back and in a panic hides the body, which now he needs us to find so he can inherit his land.

Or maybe he deliberately whacked Sietse over the head, or threw him in the Kerry River, or plugged him with the rifle farmers keep for gophers and other nuisances.

Sam had a rifle license. I had checked.

That was when I organized the search for Sietse's body, and how I'd ended up with all my muscles on fire, nursing a short glass of undiluted brandy. Had I kept a close enough eye on Sam during the search? Had I missed some marker in his behaviour that showed he knew where the body lay? Maybe his eagerness to search the last field meant something.

I thought about resuming the search and decided to wait. If Sam knew where the body lay, let him find it. Before I took half the Township out in the field again, I'd check out one more trail.

•   •   •

"I want a warrant to check his gun," I said to the sergeant on Monday morning. From the beginning of what I'd extravagantly called "the case", he'd let me do whatever I wanted. But I'd never said out loud that I thought Sietse Fennema had died of anything worse than a long walk in the cold.

He looked at me hard. "You got any evidence?"

I had to admit that evidence was a problem. "But he gets everything if the old man dies. And they had a fight just before the old guy went missing. And he's got a gun license."

"So does half the Township."

"Their fathers haven't disappeared."

He folded his arms behind his head and looked at me tolerantly. "This isn't Toronto, or *NYPD Blue*, or whatever, Tony. We gotta live here same as Sam Fennema after you get through playing detective."

He smiled. "So, yeah, you can look at his gun, but you got to ask his permission first."

• • •

All the way out to the farm I fumed. I'd phoned ahead and when I got there Sam waited in his father's bungalow, pacing from window to clock to fireplace and around again.

"You got news?" he asked.

"No. I want to check your gun for recent firing."

At first his forehead just wrinkled in puzzlement. Then it dawned on him, what I was getting at.

He stepped closer. The big hand ran through his blond hair, trembling. "You think I killed my father?"

"Just a routine check ..."

"*Verdomme* ..." The blow slammed me into the wall. Another fist, hard as a hammer, collapsed my midsection before I managed to reach a plate from the wall and smash it over his head.

Sam wasn't much of a fighter but he kept jabbing at me, his punches accompanied by a steady stream of Dutch curses.

"I thought you church boys didn't swear. Or maybe it's okay, so long's you don't do it in English?" I landed a good one right on his big mouth.

When he lunged, I reeled back into the coffee table and heard a crunch that might be the furniture or might be my bones.

But I didn't reach for the nightstick on my belt. He hadn't hit the constable, he'd hit Mike Aardehuis' kid brother. It was just Sam and me, fists and knees, mine jammed into his ribs when we rolled to the floor, boots flailing, and then his pitcher's arm reached back, grabbed my jacket and hurled me into the table from which his father's Bible went crashing to the floor.

That stopped him.

Breathing hard, he crawled to where the big book lay, face down on a litter of broken china. As he lifted it, a shower of colourful brochures drifted from between the gilt edged pages to the floor.

I picked one up. *JAMAICA SKIES — Sun and sand excursions.* His mouth open, Sam rifled through Barbados, Trinidad, Venezuela, The Bahamas. *CURACAO — FOR DAYS AND NIGHTS OF DREAM* ... Curacao made sense: one of the few Caribbean islands where Dutch is spoken. Glossy beaches, hotels, bathing beauties. Sam dropped them like his hands were on fire. He got two towels from the bathroom and threw me one. We mopped up the blood and tidied the broken dishes, set the busted furniture in a corner.

Then Sam sat heavily on the couch. He'd gotten the best of the fight but he looked the worst, ashen under his farmer's tan, eyes bleak. He told me what had really happened between him and his father.

"Yeah, I picked him up at the shelter, like you thought. I was so ticked off at him, taking off like that without telling us. At first he didn't want to come home. He actually liked it there, playing games, talking all day long."

He shook his head in disbelief. "You should have seen the place. Radios blaring. People flopped on mattresses, in the middle of the day even."

Then he remembered his own sins, and reddened. "We had another fight on the way home. I kicked him out of the truck, left him standing by the highway a mile from home."

Sam looked down, picked at his grazed knuckles. "When he didn't show up I went back to get him. But he was gone. I thought he got a ride into town and was telling the whole church what a bad son he had."

He nodded wearily towards the brochures. "If he's gone to one of those places, can you find him?"

"Do my best."

He only took one small revenge. "Still want to check my gun?" he asked.

· · ·

Five days later I drove back up Robson Road to tell Sam I had found his father.

"In Curacao?" His voice as flat as the day he'd come in to report that he'd misplaced his father. But I knew him better now, and my hearing had improved.

"Yes. Curacao. He hitchhiked into Kingston, crossed the border on the bus and flew out of New York."

"Hitchhiked."

"Yes. Then he flew to Curacao and he's been there ever since."

Sam looked down at the kitchen table, one hand covering his working mouth.

"My God. He could have been killed."

"But he wasn't, Sam. He's OK. In fact, he sounds good."

A son would see it that way, see the danger, feel the shock of finding that his father turned out to be just as big an uncertainty as the rest of life.

Myself, I was full of awe at how Sietse Fennema, the old man, had slipped the groove.

"How am I going to explain this to the church?"

"Let him explain it, if he ever comes back."

"If…?"

"He's found a nice little hotel on the coast and he's planning to stay. He says to do what you want with the farm. He won't need much to keep him going. And he'd like you to call."

I pushed a scrap of paper with address and telephone number across the table and left.

In the cruiser I sat for a few minutes pretending to scribble in my notebook. Really, I was taking a good look at the Fennema farm. A kingdom complete, with houses and barns beside a grey road lined with trees leaning in the February wind.

Then I pulled out onto the road and watched the solid lines, straight roofs and tidy fences ebbing away in the rear-view mirror.

I could see the same outline on the bank of a swollen river, an old lady rolling herself into a rowboat on a ramp of wrestled planks.

Arranging herself to face into the stream. Seizing the chance, in the middle of disaster, to go on a cruise.

The Second Battle of Crysler's Farm

The musket weighed heavy in my hands as we marched toward the rail fence, toward the dark woods and the enemy said to be lurking there. In the evening hush our black boots whumped soft on the dirt lifting puffs of dry dust, the only other sound the light jingle of buckles and bayonet blades.

I waited nervously for the sergeant's order, thinking I wouldn't recognize MacNeill. Under the stovepipe shako his big face hardened into a mask of resolve, and the order to halt rang out on a voice of steel I'd never heard.

Boots slapped together, shoulder to shoulder we stood, paying no mind to the stinging sweat on our callused hands. Then MacNeill hollered us through the 18 movements of loading and firing.

Half a beat behind the others, whose fingers knew these movements from endless practice, mine trembled on the tamping rod and I cursed under my breath wishing just once, for red-faced MacNeill's sake, to be ready.

The order to fire blasted open the door to another world, and through it the muskets roared like thunder. Bitter smoke rose above our heads, circled our hands so we could hardly see to pour the powder. But the sergeant's bellow flogged us on and we reloaded as one and fired as one. One body of green coats, black feathered hats, and long metal barrels raining smoke and thunder and death on the silent trees. Until the call, "Cease firing!" slammed shut the door of the other world.

And we were back in the summer of 1998. Our demonstration of 1812 musket drill over, enthusiastic applause erupted from the folding lawn chairs around the park.

At least, the applause looked enthusiastic. My ears rang like a carillon and for all I could tell they were patting gloved hands a hundred yards up the road.

Still in his hardass 19th century sergeant role, Howard MacNeill caught me winking at a boy in the front row and glared over his big moustache like he'd fry me alive if it could be done with historical accuracy. Those folks perched on the picnic tables had come out on a Friday night to see the Glengarry Light Infantry Fencibles, circa 1813. So we stood at attention looking military and historical while a faraway voice drifted over the dry August grass:

"Ladies and Gentlemen, this evening's demonstration of early nineteenth century firing drill is a fine example of military tactics in the War of 1812. Muskets of the period were notoriously inaccurate: the strength of an army lay in combined firepower and discipline in the field, rather than individual marksmanship."

At cop school we learned to scan a crowd without moving a muscle. What I looked for as I surveyed the few hundred history enthusiasts was any sign of the guys from my own detachment. Exchanging my OPP blues for the replica Glengarry greens was a once-in-a-lifetime, don't-ever-ask-again, favour for Howard MacNeill.

The last thing I wanted was to spend the next two years answering questions like, "So, Tony, did ya wear replica undershorts too? Did ya have camp prostitutes like in the good old days?"

But, so far so good, no one I knew had made the 48 kilometre drive from Armagh to watch us bring history to life.

"Tomorrow, Sergeant MacNeill's troops will be joined by re-enactors from across Ontario, Quebec, and the United States. On this field, they'll recreate the drama of the Battle of Crysler's Farm, an important event in local history and a turning point in the War of 1812. We expect 400 participants, all dressed and equipped for the period: if you thought the noise and smoke of this demonstration were dramatic, you haven't seen anything yet!"

Howard MacNeill's passion for noise and smoke had gotten me into this. Even back in high school he'd exploded constantly with bizarre interests and obscure bits of historical trivia. When he grew up and took over his Dad's hardware store I wasn't surprised he spent every spare minute tending his eccentric passions, of which the Glengarry Fencibles were just the summer flower.

Howard belonged to the Ontario Historical Society, the Monarchist League, the Heraldry Association. Canadian Chieftain of Clan MacNeill, he ran in every provincial and federal election for the Green Party. A big, burly guy with a walrus moustache and a generous grin, he overflowed with childlike enthusiasm that was hard work to resist.

Which was how I'd ended up here, black feather on my tall hat, musket in my hands. For five years Howard had been plotting the re-enactment of the Battle of Crysler's Farm. When Charlie Bridges, his best infantryman, came down with chicken pox Howard looked around for a replacement at just the moment I dropped into the store for a coffee and a can of varnish. His recruitment tactics were persistent, desperate, and unflattering.

"Come on, Aardehuis, you big Dutch lug. You're the same size as Charlie. You'll fit his uniform perfect."

"I'd feel like an ass, dressed up in all that rig."

"Not once you're in it. Anyway, you're used to uniforms. And guns. Our guns are bigger."

"All bang, no bullet." Those replica muskets only fired a cloud of gunpowder smoke.

But Howard didn't give up. "I know you got that weekend off. What else you planning to do with the time? Read another book? You need something real going on in your life."

I agreed that the epic history of Tony Aardehuis had drifted into a troubling lull. At 28, five years a cop, unmarried, I was still waiting for the curtain to rise on the great drama of my life. But was going back two centuries the way to "have something real going on my life"?

"And if you don't say yes, we'll be even more outnumbered than we were in 1813."

"That's supposed to be your clinching argument?"

But I already knew I would put on Charlie Bridges' uniform and carry his musket. "Just this once," I said. "Don't ask again."

Though I admit there's a bit of truth in what Howard said. I'm glad I've never used my weapon, not once in five years as a police officer. But there's a kid in all of us who likes the idea of dressing up like an old-time soldier, firing away with a big gun, and having an audience drive for miles to watch you do it. Just so long as it wasn't anyone I knew.

"Sergeant MacNeill will now dismiss his troops. Feel free to join his men on the field, ask questions about their lives as 19th century soldiers, and visit their encampment on the riverbank and check out the living accommodations."

Most of the guys loved this part, when people drifted onto the field to talk and gaze in admiration at their finery. I sidled over to Howard so he could handle the picky points of history. While he expounded on the causes of the War of 1812 to a middle-aged guy in shorts who kept pushing his glasses up his nose, a boy, maybe the guy's son, wandered over and leaned back to take a careful look at me.

About 10 years old, straw hair sticking out from under a ball cap, he took stock of me like an art student might study the "Mona Lisa".

Dark, serious eyes started at the top with the tall black shako trimmed with green cord and pewter cap badge in the shape of a silver bugle. Travelled down the dark green jacket counting three rows of metal buttons specially cast for the Upper Canada Living History Society. Noted the black pointed cuffs with turn-backs piped in white, leather cross-belt, regimental belt-plate. And came to rest on the metre long barrel light infantry musket, regarding it with reverence and desire and fear.

"You want to hold it?" I asked.

He saw I meant it, and nodded. Solemn.

"Put your arms like this," I showed him how he'd sling arms while marching cross-country so the 4.5 kilogram weight would be distributed. A sparrow has bigger arms than that kid, and the musket was twice his height. But he took it just the way I showed him, straining to hold everything it meant.

Head lifted, face warming like a lamp, I could see him feeling his way into another time. Imagining wild bush across Upper Canada. Himself tramping down the King's Road, behind the Americans as they advance on Montreal. Skirmishes and sniping and all out battle: noise and fear and screaming wounded falling around him. Wondering if he'd run or if he'd stand.

Until the spell was broken by a sharp woman's voice yammering toward us like a bossing goose.

"Terrible! Just terrible! A gun in a child's arms! After the battle we've waged to keep weapons off the toy shelves and fighting violent TV shows! This is outrageous!"

A square face under a white Tilley hat bore down on us, camera aimed and ready to snap the boy's picture with the musket cradled in his arms.

Just before the click, Howard stepped in front of the camera.

"Can I help you, madam?" he said, with his mild shopkeeper voice.

Under the iron strands of her sensible haircut she glared. "You can help by taking every last one of these weapons and melting them down."

"They're not real, madam," Howard soothed, "These muskets are all replicas. Not even required to be registered as firearms. Their purpose is solely educational, to help us remain aware of our history."

But she just sucked in a deep breath and blasted away.

"I've come from Shaughnessy, New York to protest this glorification of firearms. This event has nothing to do with history. It's a celebration of the power of the gun."

She waved her arm vaguely over us bankers, farmers, school teachers and university students sweating in our heavy wool uniforms.

"I'll bet everyone of these people belongs to the National Rifle Association."

"This is Canada, madam ..."

"Whatever."

She accused Howard, the Glengarrys, the gathering crowd, of supporting a bloodthirsty culture of violence in which innocent children and women die on a daily basis.

But she'd met her match in Howard. About the same build, square as a two car garage, they set their jaws in the same tight line and set out to talk each other into the ground.

Howard pulled hard on his moustache and lectured her and the gathering crowd on the importance of knowing your history so it can't repeat itself.

"Canada is a civil nation, madam, founded on principles of peace, order and good government. We have better gun control than the States. No capital punishment. Why don't you protest in your own backyard?"

Sympathizers rallied behind each cause. Of course the Glengarrys backed Howard, and a cluster of ladies in twill pants, Birkenstocks and humourless eyes hovered behind the outraged woman trying to get a word in edgewise. Behind them, a thin man with wire-rimmed glasses on his narrow nose blushed under the wide brim of his matching Tilley.

Only the boy paid no attention. With Charlie Bridges' musket in his arms he took a few careful steps to see if he could walk with it.

Who knows how the argument would have ended if another woman hadn't come running out of the lawn chairs waving her arms, yelling at the top her lungs, naturally headed for the largest gathering of people in uniform.

"My purse has been stolen!" she hollered in the astonished voice of crime victims everywhere, and the gun debate ended, like theory always does in the face of necessity.

But not before the lady from Shaughnessy said, "I'll be back tomorrow, with reinforcements."

By the time the police got there (a guy from the next detachment named Larry Hellerman who, of course, recognized me right away), it was clear that the purse and four or five wallets had been lifted during our demonstration. Along with a fistful of credit cards, close to a thousand dollars cash was gone.

Larry took out his notebook and jotted down names and numbers. We found a purse, empty, in the woods near our encampment. But, as Larry said, the pickpocket was likely long gone.

"It could happen again tomorrow," Howard said. "Maybe we should hire more security."

"I wouldn't worry about it," Larry told him. "They've worked this crowd. Raised suspicion. It's not likely they'll stick around."

That night we gathered around the open fire of our camp like boy scouts, except we sipped warm, homemade beer from our reproduction tin mugs.

A few early arrivals from across the border joined us, greeted like old friends by those who tomorrow would fire from opposite sides of the field. Howard shared his unease about the anti-war protest lady with a lieutenant of the American regulars who said, "We've had trouble before with her kind."

"What sort of trouble?"

"Noise mostly. Yelling and screaming over the commentary. But I heard that at the last Civil War re-enactment a bunch of them went an' lay down on the field."

Howard looked glum. "I don't know how long I been working on this. Permits, advertising, invitations … I worried about rotten weather, the goddamn dollar going up and down, regiments pulling out at the last minute. I sure as hell never worried about some crank protesting a war that happened 200 years ago."

"We've had worse though," The lieutenant said. "Bikers crashed through the gate when they re-enacted Tippecanoe in July. Roared around with a rebel flag screaming 'guts and glory'. Threw the whole battle into a shambles."

"You'd think they'd get the period right," said Howard.

"Didn't matter to them. Just so long as they could make a noise."

"We're better off with the ladies then." Howard's brow furrowed with the shrewd concentration of a military man devising strategy.

I took another sip of my yeasty beer. Like everything else eaten, worn, or touched on these weekends the brew was as authentic to the period as possible. Even the wives and children transformed themselves into 19th century camp followers, trailing their men from battlefield to battlefield. They set up white canvas tents and cooked on open fires with old pots, following 1812 recipes. Regular people, who turned into time travellers every summer weekend, loading a hundred kilograms of replica gear into vans or pickups to drive across country and set up camp in another century.

And after they'd dusted off the protester lady, even the talk around the fire was about things that happened two centuries ago.

While the beer flowed out of a huge stone crock and the children sipped apple cider, the Battle of Crysler's Farm was retold. Maybe for my benefit, the newcomer who didn't have a clue. Maybe to entertain and educate the kids whose faces glowed rapt in the flickering firelight. Maybe just because they loved to hear it themselves.

It wasn't Howard who told the story, but a guy named Arnie Robinson, a school board janitor I knew for a fact had never finished high school. But he talked this history like he wrote the book on it.

"Late fall of 1813. One year into the war, and the Americans were astonished they hadn't won yet. After they said taking Canada was just a matter of marching, they'd been fighting over a year, Canada was still

British and winter was coming on. One last chance before snowfall to make a big strike."

Flames danced in Arnie's eyes as he told about the Yankee army of 7,000 at Sacket's Harbor, across Lake Ontario from Kingston. The children groaned with satisfaction when he described the soldiers' food, the rotten meat, the doctored whisky, the bread containing traces of human shit.

"Oh gross, that's sick!"

"In late October they set out up river for Montreal, but were spotted and pursued by a small force of British regulars and militia.

"The Yankees sneaked past the guns at Fort Wellington by emptying the boats and marching the men up the river on the American side, while the boats ran past the fort in the dark. A day later 4,000 American troops were back on the Canadian side.

"The British, under the command of Lieutenant-Colonel Joseph Morrison marched with 800 men. They intended only to observe the Americans as they headed for Montreal and harass them from the rear. By the time they reached John Crysler's farm four miles from the Long Sault rapids, they were right behind the enemy.

"And then the Americans, outnumbering Morrison four to one, turned around to fight."

The fire crackled and sparked in the silence while we thought about odds of four to one, fought by men who'd slept five November nights on the cold ground. The kids leaned closer.

"Morrison promised his men 'a fair field and no favour', told his regulars they had the discipline to beat the enemy. When the Yankees came out of the woods they met the 89th, a solid line of men shoulder to shoulder firing in unison. Isaac Brock's green tigers, the 49th, wheeled in line under a hail of grapeshot to fire on American cavalry charging up the King's Road.

"With their cavalry sliced up, their big guns taken, the Americans retreated to their boats. Lost heart and gave up the advance on Montreal. Forever."

A lady in a long dress piped up, "A toast to Lieutenant-Colonel Morrison!" Which I doubt a lady would have done back then, but we raised and clinked the tin and tossed back the beer.

"What I don't understand," I said, "is why they fought so hard against the Americans. Not the British regulars, but the citizens who joined the militias. What did it matter to them what flag they lived under?"

"They knew if they stayed with the British they'd eventually get national health care," said the American lieutenant.

We laughed. Then thought seriously about the astonishing act of war. About the real men who really died at Crysler's farm.

"It was a family fight." said Howard. "Lot's of them lost their shirts in the American Revolution. Maybe they could see it all happening again, losing their land, this time without any place nearby to move, and the worst thing is all the relatives on the other side of the border saying, "told you so.""

"And thus the great Canadian nation was born," said Arnie, "rising from the ashes of sibling rivalry and a deep reluctance to hear the words, "I told you so.""

"I'll drink to that!" said a voice in the dark, and the big jug went round again.

The next morning I woke up rumpled from sleeping in my clothes, stayed grumpy after a breakfast of porridge and tea with floating leaves. One of the camp women gave me the sharp side of her tongue when she spotted my 20th century plastic razor, so I stowed it, adding the grubby feel of overnight stubble to my miseries.

By midmorning a stream of cars filled the far field where the re-enactors stashed their twentieth century vehicles, out of which poured the red tunics of British regulars, the grey homespun of Voltigeurs, Indians, and hundreds of blue-backed Americans.

And, true to her word, the protest lady filled a patch near the parking lot with twenty followers carrying hand made signs with slogans like "END THE GLORIFICATION OF WAR" and "Bread and Roses, NOT GUNS". I felt sorry for her husband who looked sadly out from under the big brim of his Tilley and held one end of the banner his wife hammered into the ground: "INTERNATIONAL WOMEN'S CRUSADE FOR PEACE".

The American lieutenant said, "Shit, why can't they go protest some real war? Let's take up a collection and buy them tickets to the West Bank."

For the next few hours platoons practised drill on the patch of soccer field called the parade ground. The hill with the best view filled with moms and dads and kids who set up chairs and blankets on the other side of a string fence. Across one section of the field we erected a makeshift rail fence to recreate the obstacles met in the battle. Inside a canvas tent the leaders of each replica regiment hashed out the battle plan, doing their best to man the forefront of the battle with regiments that had really been there in 1813.

As the crowd grew, the protesters waved their signs higher, chanting a high-pitched protest chant: "NO MORE GUNS! NO MORE WAR! NO MORE GUNS! NO MORE WAR!" Their leader stood front and centre but I had to search the throng for her husband. Didn't blame him, when I saw the white hat drifting uphill towards the main body of the audience.

The two-hour replica battle was scheduled to take place at 3:00. Until then units in turn presented displays of drill, fife and drum playing and even a tin whistle concert. In the summer sun with a thousand people gathered on the hill, coffee wagons doing brisk business, the racket of voices, drums, and cheerful whistles it felt like fair day, the thin line of protester chant threading through the din like hucksters patter. Sometimes I spotted Larry Hellerman, his OPP uniform drab in the throngs of scarlet, navy and forest green.

We Glengarrys took the field at 1:30 for a display of marching and musket drill and I managed to make it up and down the field without falling out of time. In fact I relaxed, enjoyed the attention, glad to catch sight of the boy who had held my musket near the white hat of the protester's husband. I even felt kindly disposed to those misguided ladies we almost drowned out with the tramp of our marching feet.

Until I realized another noise was doing some of the drowning. Drums, a regiment practising in the woods? But the steady growl grew louder, without rhythm. Heads in the crowd turned to look for it. The protest chorus wobbled and paused. And then five huge Harleys roared into the parking lot.

Steered in exploding circles by men who leaned back on the long seats hollering with wild grins above pirate beards, the black machines kidnapped the audience. That damn Confederate flag flapped behind the lead bike, and a mad rebel cry sliced the din of screaming engines.

Though the audience was lost, Howard kept us marching. Larry Hellerman loped through the crowd toward his cruiser and the bikes raced a tight circle around the parking lot, spitting a hail of gravel in the turns. Only the string fence prevented those maniacs from charging onto the field.

And then the lead guy caught sight of the protest ladies. Struck silent, they held the signs cautiously like they'd forgotten where they were. Except our friend from New York, who drew energy from the moment, took a step forward and held her cardboard high. Which galvanized the followers into squawking louder than ever, "NO MORE GUNS! NO MORE WAR!"

A hundred metres across the gravel the Harleys stopped, five abreast, facing the ladies. Viking arrogance glinted from their helmets in the sun, derisive teeth bared. The snarling engines revved with threat and devilry, and madmen leaned forward like an army ready to charge.

Which was when Sergeant Howard MacNeill, marching the Glengarry Light Infantry down the field of war, shouted:

"Detachment, halt!"

"Front!"

"Quick march!"

The standing engines rumbled as Howard kicked down the fence and led us off the field. What the hell's he doing, I wondered, though I obeyed the orders. Marching like the others in two lines onto the parking lot, eyes front but knowing the bikers had begun to race toward the women.

Whose faces turned pale toward the sound, so deafening I could hardly hear Howard shout from four feet ahead:

"Halt!"

A cloud of dust rose as our boots thumped to a stop.

"Ranks outward face!"

We turned, and I realized the Glengarrys were all that stood between the women and the raging machines. One line facing the protesters. Mine turned to meet the barbarians swooping down like Assyrians, Huns and Tartars with fire and cannon, grapeshot, smoke and thunder.

Straight toward us.

We stood firm. Not a man flinched as the bikes came down, red flag waving, screams of madness on the air. So close I swear I read the fine print on their tattooed arms.

And then another racket blew up on the left. Camp women in long dresses and aprons surged toward the bikers waving rolling pins and iron cooking tools, banging tin pots and shrieking like banshees. In a blur of flailing arms they advanced on the enemy.

The element of surprise is crucial in any war. The lead bike hesitated, slowed and was engulfed in a hail of flung cooking instruments, one of which bounced off his helmet with a clank. For a stunned moment he sat immobilized on his bike, then shook his head, grinned hugely and took off across the parking lot with the others in his wake.

And Larry's cruiser right behind.

• • •

As we marched back onto the field the audience applauded, not sure if the skirmish had been part of the performance. All eyes were on us, except those of the man under a white Tilley hat, who bent oddly over a lawn chair near the coffee stand.

Another wave of pot banging cut short our moment of glory. The camp women took on the protesters too, driving them from their pitch with a fierce barrage of clanking metal and flapping skirts. Enfeebled by the shock of the bikers' attack and our defence, the protesters retreated like sheep before an efficient herding dog. A few got into their cars and drove away, most joined the crowd on the hill. Two Tilley hats came together, this time on the encampment side of the hill.

For the next half hour I watched those hats, and had a quiet word with Larry when he reappeared from chasing the bikers out of town.

"You know those thefts we had yesterday?" I said.

He nodded.

"I don't know about the wife, but I'd keep a close eye on that guy with the extra-wide brimmed Tilley. Seems to me he might have quite a stash in that secret pocket."

After all that, I thought the re-enacted battle might prove a disappointment. But it did not.

We Glengarrys, with the Voltigeurs and the Indians, picked off the Americans from the woods — a good vantage point from which to watch the awesome forward march of the British regulars and, incidentally, the watching crowd when Larry Hellerman took a tall thin man with a white hat by the arm and quietly walked him toward the cruiser.

I was near the American six-pounders when the 49th advanced, then wheeled to fire on the cavalry in full view of the American guns. Above the boom of artillery and the banging muskets the orders rang clear and calm.

"Halt!"

"Cover!"

"Left wheel into line!"

"Fire by platoons from the centre to the flank!"

Through the smoke, under a hail of fire, the red tunics turned with parade ground precision, and for an instant I looked through a crack in the window of time.

Graves

The transport driver wasn't happy when I stopped the traffic for Mrs. Laura Ames. After the air brake hiss he idled there, tapping on the accelerator so the engine grumbled for him. Behind him, highway traffic backed up a hundred yards and around the bend, and then the silver hearse passed through the parted Red Sea at a stately crawl.

Every funeral escort I do, I marvel at the courtesy paid the dead. It's kind of touching, like finding out that grown-ups still know all the rules to hide-and-seek. I'd pulled up in the middle of the highway, stopped the travel of people going about their business. At first you could feel the edgy worry, because who knows what that damn cop is doing there. He could be shutting down the road for hours. The truck driver checked his mirrors for any escape, a way to turn and try another road. A few cars actually did a three-point turn and scooted off.

Then the funeral procession glided into view and everyone relaxed. Even the trucker stopped yelling at me with his gas pedal, sat back and took the time to polish his sunglasses.

Mrs Laura Ames read the board in the window of the hearse. She was followed by the limo with the nearest and dearest: grown son and the grieving husband who might have been expected to die before his ten-years-younger wife.

I knew most of the families rolling through the intersection at a respectful 15 km/h. The Regional Chair, here because Mr. Ames was once mayor of Armagh, hunched over the wheel with the effort of travelling close but not too close. The minister, with my friend Howard MacNeill riding in his car. Then those who've come just for

Laura Ames, because she was well liked, a volunteer at the library, at the hospital, and a member of every ladies group in town.

Finally the tail of the long procession appeared round the bend and not the last, but almost the last, was Owen Debrett. His bashed-up little truck, empty and maybe even hosed down for the occasion, scuffed through the intersection and I waved the grumbling transport through.

Duty done, I could have turned the cruiser back to town, but it was one of those crisp September mornings that make you think the papers on your desk can wait. And anyway, this was Howard's debut as a graveside bagpiper. And besides, I owed Mrs. Ames an apology.

Just last week she'd been puttering around the library in her pearls and volunteer smock, pushing her grey hair back and rambling on about the books I'd chosen.

"You boys always were interested in history," she said, scrutinizing the brand-new copy of *Rebel Winds — The Rising of Upper Canada*. "Howard MacNeill made us order this book."

It wasn't being called a boy. At her age anyone under 50 probably looked young. It was just wanting, after a day blitzing traffic on the 401, to get home, shower, pour a Rebellion lager to go with the new book, and that nice Mrs. Ames just wouldn't stop talking. Started on some relation of hers who'd been related to someone else who'd written a book on Isaac Brock.

Not the same war.

I didn't say it, just waited for my chance. When she said, "I've got just the book for you …" and disappeared beneath the counter, I took it. She was still talking when the door closed behind me.

So I parked at the gate of the cemetery, doffed my Stetson and joined the sombre mourners at the grave.

I've seen sadder funerals. After all, even if the heart attack took everyone by surprise, she was 71. Her son, owner of Armagh Chev-Olds and rumoured to be thinking of following the old mayor into politics, stood beside his father. Mr. Ames looked older and shakier than the wife he was burying and his hand trembled when he dropped a clump of daisies on the coffin. Then, while Howard piped through "Flowers of the Forest", the box descended, and the minister invited everyone back to the church hall for a light lunch.

Awkward silence. The crowd splintered, headed for the cars. Mr. Ames stood a long minute looking down after his wife, wiping the wet off his face. Finally the son plucked him by the elbows and he shuffled off toward the limousine.

"Catch a ride back?" asked Howard.

"Sure."

But I didn't move because I couldn't take my eyes off the last mourner by the open grave. Owen Debrett, washed and shaved, hair ragged but firmly combed. Not in a suit, but still a good try. Tweed jacket. Belt that skipped a loop so the grey flannel trousers (wrong by only a size or two) listed south at the hip. I'd never seen him so presentable. How old now? Fifty? Fifty-five? It was 20 years since he'd picked up odd jobs on my Dad's farm and I'd tagged behind as he went about his work.

Owen stared into the grave, stone faced. Then he turned, tramped back to his truck and drove away.

"What's he doing here?"

"You don't know?" Howard's big face spread with disbelief.

"Know what?"

"She was his mother."

Mostly I think I know all about the place I grew up; then I step on an old sore or a story covered by silence and I'm the immigrant kid again.

"Mrs. Ames was Owen Debrett's mother?"

"First marriage," Howard nodded. "One time the Debretts were a big family around here. His father was Lloyd, Floyd Debrett. Something like that. He was the last of the family and went off to the war right after he married Laura Ames. Owen was born after his father died."

Howard stopped packing up the pipes to think about it. "There's something hushed up about him. Died in the war but you won't find his name on the memorial. No one talked about him."

"I'll say."

Howard grinned. "She was well-liked, though," he continued, "so people didn't mention it. Then she married Richard Ames. My dad said she was his sweetheart first anyway, and that was that. She got a nice turnout, eh?"

All the way back to town Howard, deep in love with his new computer and the internet, yapped about some web site he'd found for Clan MacNeill. I made the right noises, but couldn't get away from that picture of Owen glaring down into his mother's grave. Owen Debrett, local drunk and general loser, son of the lady in pearls.

"Hey," said Howard, "I got onto the census records. You know your family has the only Aardehuis name in Canada?"

"Amazing."

"Yeah, lots of other weird handles, though: Aandezande, Apelkoortje …"

"So, Owen was the mayor's son?"

He stopped mangling the Dutch names. "Stepson. I still can't believe you didn't know that."

"If no one told you, would you connect them? I mean, you got Charles there, Mr. Retail Sales, next in line for Parliament. Then there's Owen picking over the garbage dump."

"I suppose we just got used to it. Maybe he just didn't take to the stepfather. Now, the National Archives, there's a treasure chest …"

I dropped him off at his hardware store and turned down the offer of lunch. Howard in the first flush of a new enthusiasm can be strong drink and I'd heard enough about web sites for one day. Then I cleared for a break with dispatch and turned the cruiser toward Kerry Township and the concession road behind my father's farm. Why?

Because it was a nice day for a drive and I was still itching with curiosity and puzzlement by that graveyard scene.

Before I was old enough to help my Dad, Owen Debrett appeared at his side for spring planting and fall harvest. At five, I only saw the way he could bring the seed drill round with the casual swing of his arm. Perched on the tractor fender I rode beside him up and down the fields, hypnotized by the wind and the roaring engine. I watched him stop in the middle of a turn, climb down to move a kildeer nest to the margin of the seed drill's swath. Using a shovel so the frantically keening mother would not find her eggs contaminated.

At 10, I understood how different he was from other men. In a three metre trailer set at a random angle on his back road lot, he lived among broken cars, cannibalized trucks and tractors, wringer washers and stoves retrieved from the dump. We'd ride our bikes past on the gravel road, fascinated by the junk and the outrageous disorder, but we never stopped because of the dogs. The number of Owen's dogs could never be pinned down. They sprawled on car seats or under the trailer and their shadows stirred among the rusting appliances. If they barked, Owen appeared, shirtless, at the door. He'd tell them to be still, then raise one hand to us while the dogs watched with yellow eyes and lolling tongues.

• • •

The dogs, or their grandsons and daughters, were still there when I pulled into Owen's yard. I knew he was home because of the pickup but there was no sign of him as I climbed out of the cruiser and the dogs stood up.

Seven that I could see. Maybe more among the wrecks. The biggest was black with wiry fur, tall as a Shepherd, one ear torn and saucer eyes like the dog in the Grimm story that scared the pants off me when I was six.

"Hello, boys." I said, one hand resting lightly on my can of pepper spray. I called toward the open door of the trailer, "You home, Owen?"

No reply.

"It's Tony Aardehuis. Saw you at the funeral and thought I'd stop by."

Silence. I took a step toward the trailer.

The dogs didn't move but a seven throated growl warned me to stop.

"I just want to see the boss," I told them, reasonably. "Just to check if he's okay."

They thought about it.

I took another step. The one-eared dog put his head down, the hackles came up and I was thinking that retreat might be wiser when a gruff voice called, "It's all right, sons."

The dogs and I looked at Owen leaning in the doorway. He still wore the graveyard clothes but the tie had shifted north and the grey pants were stained at the knee.

"I just came by to express condolences."

"Well, that's very kind. You're the first." Under the untrimmed beard the smile broke at one end into sadness. He said, "You were always a good kid."

He turned abruptly, reached back into the trailer for an open mickey of Five Star and splashed the bottle in my direction. "I'm having a light lunch after the funeral," he said, "Care to join me?"

"Another time."

"Hold you to it."

"She was a nice lady." I offered.

"Yeah, she was," As if drinking a toast, he took a long pull, then wiped the beard down with an open hand. "She never did me anything but good. Only that she married that piss-poor excuse for a man ... "

Another pull on the bottle and a long stare over the cab of a broken truck. "She was so good to everyone. But she could never say no to him. Now she never will. It was the one bad turn and it cancelled out all the rest."

Then he came back to now. He grinned and showed a blackened tooth but this time the smile was the real thing. "You always was a boy with a million questions, Tony. Still got that big nose, eh?"

"Just wanted to check if you were all right."

"Oh, we're all right. I'm not going to shoot myself."

His place, disappearing in the rearview mirror, was a mess. Broke every by-law on the books and no doubt the Township wrung it's hands and pestered him to clean up from time to time. But no one ever tried to shift him. Last winter they sent me on a course to Toronto and I saw Owen's beard, black teeth and unfocused eyes looking back at me from a hundred doorways. On the whole, I thought we managed better in Armagh.

•　•　•

Then I went back to work and Owen Debrett did not cross my mind again till five days later I'm called off the highway because he's raising hell in a lawyer's office.

"What's he done?" I asked dispatch.

"Property damage. Uttering. No weapons."

No weapons.

J.J. Taylor ran a one-lawyer office on the main street above the men's wear store. A small crowd mumbled on the sidewalk and the secretary waited at the bottom of the stairs taking jerky puffs on a cigarette.

"Debrett just went nuts," she said. "The dad and Charles were there to read Mrs. Ames' will. In he comes with that wolf of his and all of a sudden there's yelling, the French door to the office got smashed. Then Mr. Taylor's telling me to call the police. So I did and then I got out fast as I could."

The wide oak stairs creaked all the way up. I paused in front of the frosted glass door where gold letterring read *J. J. Taylor, Barrister & Solicitor*. What I knew about J.J. Taylor was that he drew up my Dad's partnership papers with my brother and every November he was the Legion guy who lay the wreath at the cenotaph. I swung the door open slowly, calling out that the police had arrived.

"We're over here," said a quiet voice down the hall.

I walked toward the splash of broken glass on the carpet, stepped into the open doorway and found them sitting so still they could have been sitting for a painting: "Reading the Will", or maybe, "The Black Sheep".

All brown and sombre colours: lawyer with patient hands folded on an oak desk facing the upright son who sat with one comforting hand on his old father's arm. Chair pulled as far as possible from the family failure clad in coveralls stiff with dirt and an odour of sweat and unwash you couldn't put in any painting.

No weapons.

It wasn't the exact truth. Beside Owen, saucer eyes fixed huge and unwavering on old Mr. Ames, sat the one-eared dog. At the sight of me, Charles, the car dealer, half rose in his chair and said, "Thank God!"

A low, deep growl rumbled in the throat of the black dog.

"He won't let us go," said Charles but he sat down fast.

It seemed they'd been sitting here, motionless, watching Owen while his dog watched them. Watching and waiting.

I stepped into the room and stood, suspended, when the dog growled again and bared its yellow teeth.

"It's okay, son," said Owen. The dog subsided and I took a chair by the door. Next to Owen. Facing the tableau of lawyer, dutiful son, and aged father.

"What's going on, Owen?"

Today his eyes were sharp and clear. He said, "There's something wrong here. There's something been hid."

"Something wrong with your mother's will?"

"Something wrong with the whole setup. The whole last 50 years."

"You're out of your mind." The half brother, a slow learner, tried again to rise but the dog stood too, dark hair rising on the scruff of his neck.

"Do something with that damn dog."

"Owen," I said, trying to ignore the rest of them. "What started this?"

He opened his mouth to start, then turned and nodded at the lawyer.

"The will itself is straightforward," said John Taylor, lines puzzling his forehead. "Most of her assets were in common with her husband. There were some particular bequests: jewellery mostly. Garnet ring for Charles, pearls for his wife." He steepled his fingers, paused. "Then there's an investment certificate Mrs. Ames left to Owen. Held in both their names, containing funds received as a widow's pension on the death of her first husband, with interest accumulated since 1945. It'd be about $50,000 now."

It looked like a windfall, a new trailer for the backroad lot, a new pickup truck, a secure supply of dog food. Not something that would make a man smash a window. John Taylor looked perplexed and we all thought about it.

Finally, I said, "Sorry, Owen, I don't get it."

He said, "The only pension my father would have got was a military pension."

"So?"

He looked steadily at Mr. Ames, his stepfather, who gazed up and away, eyes fixed on a spot high above the lawyer's head.

Owen said, "Lloyd Debrett. No one ever said his name. It was like he never existed. One time I'm sitting in church and I read the list of soldiers on the wall. There's no Debrett there either. Like he never existed. So I ask and I'm told my father's name wasn't there because he was shot as a deserter. Not to be mentioned for the hurt it would do my mother."

In John Taylor's eyes the light went on. "I see."

We turned to look at him. He said, "A deserter doesn't get a military pension."

"What the hell difference does it make?" exploded Charles. "There's $50,000 in that account. You should be damn grateful. Bloody fuss about nothing."

"Nothing?" Owen's voice had a dangerous edge to it and the dog's good ear twitched. "You can burn the money. I want the truth about my father. I want it *known*. Drummer here's not letting anyone out of this room until I know."

"You putting up with this?" Charles leaned toward me, indignation stretching the shoulders of his suit coat. "You got pepper spray, you got a gun."

"Make one move and Drummer will rip your throat out," said Owen calmly. "Or he can babysit while I go down and get the gopher gun out of the truck." At the mention of his name the dog stood taller, tongue hanging out so that he looked almost friendly.

"You sit there and keep your mouth shut." I said to Chev-Olds. "We can take care of this, Owen, right here. No problem. We find out about your father's military service and you let everyone go. That's the deal, right, Owen?"

It's hard to say who he saw when he looked at me. Cop in uniform. The guy who called the day his mother lay down in the ground. The kid perched beside him on the fender of a tractor. But he nodded, and I had nothing to lose.

"No matter what we find out."

He nodded again, with trace evidence of a smile, "I just want to know."

"Then I need to use the phone to call Howard MacNeill. You know Howard, from the hardware? He'll know how to find out."

Owen passed the phone and, for all he lived in a shack, knew enough to say, "Use the speaker phone."

It took about 10 rings before Howard picked up and his voice boomed "MacNeill's" into the echo of the room.

"Can you drop the store for a minute?" I figured there was no point pretending I was just passing the time. He might as well understand what was going on. "I've got a situation here, a little urgent. I'm in John Taylor's office with Owen Debrett. Owen says he's going to do some damage if he doesn't find out about his father's military record. Can you help me out?"

"No problem." Howard understood the need, I could tell. All the same, there was a shade of vindicated eccentric in that voice I knew I'd pay for later. "You got a computer there? On the net?"

Taylor swung in his chair, flicked on his monitor.

Howard said, "Let's start with the Archives."

Taylor tapped at the keys and I moved to look over his shoulder.

"National Archives," Howard talked us through. "You see that? Click on *Military records.*"

We were right behind him, scanning the options: *Boer War. Canadian Expeditionary Force 1914-1918.*

"Sorry, Owen. Nothing for your dad's war." Long pause. "Let's try Veterans' Affairs"

More clattering keys, more clicks. We followed Howard through the government maze, landed on something called the *Canadian Virtual War Memorial.*

"Type in 'Debrett'."

Like he couldn't help it, Owen stood and moved closer, arms held tight across his chest. The others looked like they might come too but Drummer showed them his big smile and they subsided into the chairs.

The drive hummed and the screen flipped to a page that told us, "No record. Try searching again."

Over the phone line we could hear Howard breathing, thinking. Owen moved from foot to foot, eyes fixed on the words: "No Record".

"Let's try some links," said Howard. "You know his regiment, Owen?"

"No."

Like he knew the air in this room was strung tight as wire, Howard talked and muttered, filling the silence with the illusion of possibility, a faint likelihood that somewhere: *museums, collections, first World War, Korean war, peacetime forces,* somewhere there was a record for the one forgotten man.

"He died in the war?"

"Yes."

"Bingo. He's got to be buried someplace. Try the *Commonwealth War Graves Commission.* See that? Down there at the bottom."

In seconds we faced a screen that told us: *Their Name Liveth Forevermore. To search the register click here.*

It gave us a page of blanks, a question waiting to be sent.

John Taylor's fingers hovered above the keys and then for some reason he turned to Owen and said, "Here. You do it."

Slowly, like he was walking up to a witness box, Owen took the chair and hesitantly finger pecked the surname: "Debrett". First Initial: "L". Year of death: "Unknown". Force: "Unknown". Nationality: "Canada".

"Click *Search*." said Howard. There was no time to wish before the screen kicked back, "Sorry, your inquiry did not find any information …".

The silence hurt.

I watched Owen's mask of face for signs he might go back on his bargain. The dog watched us. The old man watched the hands trembling in his lap.

Chev-Olds couldn't stand it anymore. "Dammit, enough's enough. This is bloody forcible confinement."

Howard said, "You sure about that first initial, Owen?"

"What about nationality?" said John Taylor, like he's into the hunt now as much as anyone. "At the Legion we have some guys who served with the Brits. It said on that first screen they'd be listed by country of service."

Howard said, "So try again under *UK & Former Colonies.*"

Owen didn't move, so I leaned over him, made the change and this time the hour glass hovered in front of us like hope and finally a single line appeared:

"DEBRETT L. O."

Owen sucked in a deep breath.

"Go," said Howard, "Click on the name. I'm just a step ahead, Owen. It's all on the next screen."

And there it was:

In memory of Lloyd Owen Debrett, Flight Sergeant,
Air Gunner 103 Squadron, Royal Air Force, who died
January 10th, 1945, age 22.
Commemorative Information: Fransward Village Cemetery,
Friesland, The Netherlands. Near the southeastern corner of

the cemetery are the graves of two airmen belonging to the
Royal Air Force.
Record of Commemoration: Flight Sergeant Lloyd Owen Debrett,
husband of Laura Debrett, Armagh, Ontario, Canada.
Remembered with Honour.

"Can I come over for the champagne?" said Howard.

"Remembered with honour."

There was pain and awe and gratitude in Owen's voice, and he
couldn't take his eyes off the words. Drummer, deserting his post,
went straight to him and shoved the dark snout into his lap.

"How the hell did you pull this off for 50 years?" John Taylor,
Legion man, looked at the former mayor like he'd crawled out from
under a rotten board.

Mr. Ames answered so quiet you could hardly hear.

"She was mine first. And then, even though he had her, he left her
behind. Had to go be the big hero." Fifty-years-old, the bitterness was
still strong enough to sour his mouth and the wattled chin lifted
defiantly. " I used to drop in, help her with the chores. So I was there
when the telegram came. In those days a government telegram meant
one thing. She was terrified. Her hands were shaking so, she gave it to
me to read. You know what it said." His withered hand waved at the
smoke of the past, but it was real now and couldn't be brushed aside.

"I knew I'd stand a better chance if he wasn't put on a pedestal. So
I told her he'd been shot as a deserter. Then I burned it."

"And the pension?"

His smile thinned. "What does a woman know about pensions?"

Owen, absently stroking the big dog, did not even look at him, he
was so full. Full and brimming over with knowing.

Of course Charles, thick as a brick, insisted I arrest Owen and
rhymed off 10 charges he could think of. Then he looked to the lawyer
for backup.

John Taylor's voice was dead even, like he was talking stocks and
mutual funds. "I understand you're considering a run at town counsel,
Charles. The Ames name has always been good in Armagh."

• • •

So that was how we left it. Owen got his $50,000 and a small piece of himself back. Richard Ames was buried a couple months later beside his beloved wife.

But one afternoon Howard and I drove out to the concession road behind my father's farm. Nothing had changed, except maybe another dog crawled out from under the trailer. We told Owen we had something he should see, and Drummer came along for the ride, his big tongue wetting up the back seat, but he had to stay outside when we got to the Presbyterian Church.

It was dim in there but not so you couldn't read the names on the plaque below the gilt-edged words, "let us now praise famous men and our fathers who begat us ..."

Owen swallowed hard. "Who paid for that?"

Maybe he didn't want to be owing to his stepbrother. Maybe he thought it was the church or the Legion or someone else he should thank.

"My Dad." I told him. "Your father's buried in Holland. Now we're here. He thought it was only right."

Then we stood for a minute looking at the last gold-lettered name shining just a shade brighter and not dimmed by time.

A Good Heart

"You're out of your mind," I told Howard MacNeill when I ran into him in the courthouse hallway. "You stick up for that guy, this town will never forget it."

"He called me," said Howard. My friend is so big the crowd of lawyers, clerks and harried relatives searching for the right bail court divided around him like waves on a coastal rock. Above the big beard his eyes were tired, like he'd been up all night making calls, and I kicked myself for not getting to him first.

"You knew they arrested him?" he asked.

I nodded. "I was there."

"Oh." His wide face didn't change expression, just looked at me steadily, as if just now was he remembering that I'm a cop.

"It'll stand up, Howard." I told him. "Sexual exploitation and manufacturing child pornography; that's what he's charged with."

The big shoulders lifted, almost apologetically. "He didn't do it, Tony. I know the guy." As if that should be enough. "I know the guy."

"So what. Why you? Let his principal come to the rescue. Or his union."

"I'm his friend. He called me."

That's when I first heard it, trumpet flourish or maybe bagpipes warming up: the signal sound of Howard MacNeill with his mind made up, riding to the rescue of the last lost cause. Long as I've known him he's walked his own trail, and Howard is nothing if not loyal. I should know; he's the only one, friend or family, who visited me at every posting I've worked in my brief career with the OPP. I should have remembered he was Joe Menzies' friend too.

"You're off your tack," I said, and then the courtroom doors swung open.

Seven parts damn fool, I thought, taking my seat behind the Crown. MacNeill's Hardware has been a fixed point in the small town universe of Armagh for five generations but the world is changing and Home Depot is moving closer all the time. Till now, habit and a liking for Howard, a kind of genial amusement at his 49 eccentric hobbies and his willingness to shoot the breeze any day on any topic have kept my friend in business.

But this would cross the line. Standing along side a teacher with those charges, pornography, sexual abuse, no way would that go down in Armagh. In spite of everything we'd found at his place I still had my own lingering doubts about Joe Menzies' guilt, but just then I was more worried about keeping Howard out of the line of fire. Sitting there in the bail court, waiting for the weekend arrests to be brought in from the cells, I thought about how even this morning, in the **Two x Four Diner**, I could feel the storm brewing. Eight AM, and Laurie leaned across the scratched glass counter eager for news.

"Hey, Tony," she said, "I hear you guys arrested Mr. Menzies."

A bright girl, she'd finished high school last spring. Now she poured coffee and lifted donuts between thin sheets of paper while she saved for university. When she asked about Joe Menzies fear and hunger and the relief of a terrible boredom glittered in her mascara crusted eyes. Around the table the shopkeepers, warming up for the rush in downtown Armagh, lifted their heads to listen. Other mornings, on the way to the detachment, I've joined them to hash over last night's game or the up and down dollar, or we'd listen to Howard MacNeill chewing over some nonsense in the paper.

This morning he hadn't been there. I should have known where he'd be.

"Coffee to go, Laurie. Double cream, no sugar. Where'd you hear that?" I wasn't surprised the word had spread, just tracking the pattern.

"My uncle lives around the corner from him. Said you guys carried boxes and boxes out of his house last night. So it's a porn charge, right? What was as he into? Boys or girls?"

At the table the stirring spoons stopped, cigarettes hovered in mid air.

"You hear what the weather was going to be?"

"Sunny and mild. Come *on*, Tony, I was in his class last year." Laurie passed the styrofoam across and leaned closer. "I *never* would'a guessed he was bent."

"Give it up, Laurie," said Fred Clarke from the service station, "Tony won't say anything. Too damn professional for that."

I just smiled at Fred, who is about five foot four, the best fly fisherman in Ontario, and a feisty article to get out of a bar on a Saturday night. Searching for change in the pocket of my uniform, I asked Laurie, "So, what novel are they studying these days?"

"*Heart of Darkness.*"

Fred, like he was telling me the time for pick-up hockey'd been changed, said, "If that bastard touched any kids, he's dead."

I pretended not to hear, just put down a toonie, took the coffee, and ran.

On the way to the courthouse I passed the *Welcome to ARMAGH (Population 2,018)* sign, at the edge of town. Then the water tower with a slogan painted on by the service clubs: *Hometown with a Good Heart.* Outside the cruiser windows Armagh passed like a tourist film of postcard pretty small town Ontario basking in October sun, dappled with the gold of falling leaves. The IGA, the post office, the memorial to the glorious dead. A place people moved so their kids could grow up safe.

When the word got out that one of the teachers at the high school had been arrested on these charges the nice mothers and fathers of Armagh would feel disbelief, then a twist in the gut. And then, rage.

Just the pattern I'd followed when Sergeant Carr asked if I thought Joe Menzies could be a kid banger.

"No way. Best teacher I ever had." My insides had lurched at the thought, my mind ran through every newspaper article I'd ever read about men who were falsely accused of sexual abuse. Then I watched Sergeant Carr's interview with Ryan Boyd.

"Magazines. First he showed them to me," said the boy while he tugged at the blond spikes of hair standing on his head like nails.

Right away he brought to mind a couple of kids I'd dealt with in my last posting, not long ago when I was 25, fresh in the field when first impressions still hit hard. I'd gone with a Children's Aid worker to seize two sisters after a doctor said someone, maybe the father, had been at them. Those kids wouldn't meet your eye; but the next thing you know you're prying them out of your lap. Every move they made was part fear, part apology, part invitation.

Ryan Boyd laughed like those girls, with a knife-edge underneath, and he had the same dodgy eyes and twitching hands. Fifteen, the Sergeant said. He looked about 12, small for his age and his voice hadn't broken.

"Magazines. Was that at school?" Carr asked.

"No. At his house." Ryan picked between his fingers, then shifted in so close Carr's chair scraped back. "That was where he, like, did it."

"Did it?"

"Yeah, the pictures."

Ryan's eyes slid off, wandering till they focussed, blue and anxious on the mirror we stood behind.

"I'll kill the bastard," said the man who stood beside me. Derek Purcell, Ryan's uncle. Big guy, worked the municipal snow plow in winter, drove tractor cutting grass along the side roads in summer so he smelled like the outdoors and the wind. Ryan's dad had left long ago. His mother was laid up forever with arthritis or something. Derek Purcell, heavy jowls set grim under an Armagh Motors cap, was the one who'd brought Ryan in to make the complaint.

Later, Carr asked him, "You think there was more people involved?"

"Not that I know of." said Derek Purcell. "But that don't mean there ain't."

● ● ●

In the bail court the door to the custody hall opened and three men were put into the prisoners' box. Only 16 hours since he opened his front door to our search warrant and Joe Menzies already looked like a changed man. Shrunken, a withered copy of the teacher who had once showed me how to scan a sonnet. There'd been no sleep for him and he wore the sweatshirt and jeans he'd been arrested in, and, at 168 centimetres, was dwarfed by the tall men on either side. The first night in jail is hard no matter who you are; for a 55-year-old teacher with a heart attack behind him, a small man held on the least popular charge you could carry into a cell it must have been a nightmare. He lifted the handcuffs to push the hair out of his eyes and a bruise showed on his arm, another on the side of his face. Neither had been there when I brought him down to the cells.

"Good work," murmured the man beside me and I realized trouble, in the form of Derek Purcell, had joined us. Victims and their families have a right to be there every step of the way, but most don't show for a bail hearing. I glanced around and was relieved to see Howard sitting near the back. With any luck Purcell would never know he'd been here.

Most people, in court for the first time, show some awe at the power and peculiarities of the place. When the clerk said her "All rise" and the Justice came in Purcell barely lifted his backside off the bench, and, while Crown and Duty Counsel worked the first prisoner (driving impaired), he sat there with his big arms crossed, chawing away on a wad of gum like he was trying hard to hold in his feelings about what had been done to his nephew. Like he was going to make sure we got it right.

Behind the Plexiglas Menzies sat on the bench, staring ahead like he didn't want to know who might be there to see him in this fix. Only when he stood for his own bail hearing did the tired eyes skid beyond the foreground of lawyers, move over the watching public, and catch for an instant on Purcell.

The look snagged for just a second while the Crown read the information and informed the court that the defendant had no record, also no matters outstanding before the courts; and Duty Counsel said a surety was ready to be presented and I wondered what poor relative had been sucked into coming to his rescue. Then Menzies' eyes lifted away from Ryan's uncle with a new tension, a new clench to the pallid, unshaven jaw.

Who could tell what threat Purcell had managed to get across the empty air?

Who could blame him?

Then the lawyer asked the surety to take the stand and a damned fool named Howard MacNeill stood up.

Purcell shifted beside me, trying to take this in. He'd been buying his hammers and nails and paint cans at MacNeill's Hardware forever and here's the man stepping forward on behalf of the sick bastard who abused his nephew? The chawing mouth bit harder, faster. The rest of the proceedings could hardly have meant a thing to him. Without a record it was a given that Menzies would be bailed, and he was, at $5,000, no deposit. The usual restrictions and some extra: show his face at the detachment twice a week; stay away from kids under eighteen; be of good behaviour and keep the peace.

Then the court moved on to a car theft, Menzies closed his eyes and leaned back against the wall, and Derek Purcell looked like a very unhappy man.

• • •

This was how the lines of belief and disbelief would fault the town, and nothing would be like it was before yesterday afternoon when everyone on King Street stopped to wonder where our three OPP cruisers might be heading in the shimmering sun of a bright October afternoon. Every eye that saw us, up King, down David and finally onto Mill, the oldest and prettiest street in Armagh, formed a theory about where we were going.

Rob Robson, the least perturbable constable in the OPP took his eyes off the road for a split second to glance across at me. "My sister's boy was in this fellow's class," he said.

"My nephew too." I didn't like the way his hands flexed on the wheel, or the worried bite of his bottom lip, so I added, "So was I, about a dozen years ago."

Then we pulled up in front of Menzies' house.

Victorian cottage: one story, board and batten, gingerbread trim, white picket fence. The perfect little house for a single guy, and until now it had fit right into the neighbourhood. That changed the instant we parked the cruisers and walked up the sidewalk. Across the street two boys jumped off a tire swing and closed in for a better look. The loans manager at the bank stopped raking leaves to watch. A passing car slowed.

When he opened the door Joe Menzies had stood there in after-school clothes, jeans and a sweatshirt, a bottle of Wellington's County Ale in his hand. A beer to which Howard had also introduced me.

"Oh," the teacher said, like he was trying to figure out why six officers would be crowding his little porch. "This is about the kids?"

In his late-50s, a shrivelled version of the teacher I remembered, maybe because of the heart trouble I'd heard about. His grey hair needed a cut and I thought: pitiful, a shrunken old man trying to look young and radical. In the background, classical music thundered like we were in a movie and the heavy scene came next.

"Warrant to search these premises ..." Sergeant Carr thrust the papers into Menzies' hand and shoved past him. "Start in here!" he barked, waving toward the livingroom. "Bookshelves, top to bottom. Michelle, take the computer."

Menzies backed out of our way, then stood in the open doorway with his mouth half open. He lifted the warrant papers with a shaking hand and read, or pretended to read. Then he just watched, a look on his face like if he could just concentrate he'd be able to figure out what was going on. After a few minutes he looked out where the neighbours had begun to gather and carefully set the ale on a table and pulled the door closed.

No sign that he remembered me from English 4A1, Room 103, under the stairs.

After he punched the CD player into silence the only sounds were Michelle, the technical expert, clicking away on the keyboard and us thumping books on and off of the shelves. Rows of Trollope, Gaskell, Elliot. I shook for loose papers, read the inscriptions, shoved them back.

You don't like to search and find nothing, but after an hour I was hoping maybe we wouldn't. Maybe we'd been conned by the boy with spiky hair. Maybe he didn't like his mark on the last little quiz.

Carr paced from room to room. After an hour Menzies looked calmer, like he'd found the design. Maybe, after all, there was nothing to it.

You'd think we'd be glad.

"Tony," said Carr, "Shift to the bedroom."

I lifted the mattress of a slatted mission-style bed. Rifled through flannel shirts and boxes of school papers on the closet shelf. How could this guy teach here for 20 years without anyone ever knowing what he's up to? He'd taught me, my brother Mike, now Mike's boy and my nephew Jonas. Could we be that wrong? Hadn't I told Carr he was the best teacher I ever had?

You'd have thought such a small man would have trouble handling a high school class. Even 10 years ago, at 17, I'd been a head taller than the weird little teacher who was supposed to have had poetry published in some magazine no one ever heard of. But the word on Mr. Menzies was good, the ruling in his favour:

"Not a book he hasn't read.

"Got a tongue like a razor.

"No, like a machete.

"Never know what the guy's going to pull next."

From the bedside table I lifted a copy of *Broken Ground*, the book Howard gave all his friends last Christmas and I remembered how Menzies once assigned the last 16 lines of "Ulysses" for memorization.

"Know it by heart, tomorrow."

Over our groans he'd begun the long poem from the beginning. Halfway through Howard jabbed me with his elbow, whispered: "Check it out. The bugger's not looking at the book."

After our teacher had recited the whole 70 lines, how could we complain about 16?

While I rummaged through the shelf below the window I wondered if any of that Tennyson still mumbled somewhere in my head.

> "... Come, my friends.
> 'Tis not too late to seek a newer world.
> Push off, and sitting well in order smite
> the sounding furrows ..."

"Anything?" said Carr from the doorway, and I got up so fast my head bashed the bookshelf.

Had I said it out loud?

The sergeant stood there chewing on his moustache, looking tense, not wondering whether to send me for counselling.

"Not yet."

"Sergeant?" called Michelle from the computer.

We gathered around the screen, talking low.

Michele said, "The kid claims he got emails from him?"

"Yeah."

"There's nothing here. No text at all. No files. Nothing in the recycle bin."

Carr nodded heavily.

"But the kid *is* listed in the address file."

The sergeant brightened. "Okay. So there's something here. Some place. We just have to find it."

He was right. Ten minutes later at the bottom of the woodbox on the enclosed back porch Rob found a cache of photographs: Ryan Boyd in 29 poses on a slatted mission-style bed.

"It's a mailbox," said Carr, jerking his chin at the crate of firewood. "We've seen it before. Out on the porch, easy access. Someone picks up, someone drops off, a regular goddamn circulating library."

"So there are others," said Rob, heavily.

"Oh, yeah, there are others."

When Carr arrested him Menzies' face pasted into grey, but he didn't flinch. The only protest came when I got the cuffs out and he said, "That is certainly not necessary."

And he was right, if you thought the cuffs were to keep him from running away. He didn't get it. He didn't understand that the first sentence comes before the trial, when he's walked out to the cruiser, along the picket fence and down the line of his neighbours' eyes.

• • •

It would take an hour to process a bail release. For Howard's sake I stuck around and watched the cluster of reporters gather on the steps around Derek Purcell and the Crown. Local radio, cable TV and the weekly paper; even two stringers for Toronto and Montreal looking for filler on a slow news day. Because a teacher or a priest or a doctor gone bad is always an easy sell, and in Eastern Ontario we'd had more than our share.

"Never should'a been let go," Purcell said, doing the outraged relative. "Not fair on the kids who got to see him walking around town."

I pictured Howard walking into this bear pit, pictures in the newspapers with Menzies beside him, looking like a weasel. Purcell's good ol' boy indignation sharpening the contrast. So I got Howard's keys, parked his car near the canteen delivery door, and met them when they stepped out of the bail room.

Looking even greyer than he had in the box, Menzies took the stairs slowly, gripping the rail tight, his face shining with sweat.

"You look like hell," said Howard. "I'm taking you to the hospital."

Menzies said, "Screw that. I just want to get home."

He wouldn't put his head down or hide himself in anyway, but we were lucky. A catering truck stopped on the street and reporters who hadn't abandoned their posts for an hour missed the moment.

"Thanks, Tony," said Howard as we swung out of the parking lot and were gone.

"Tony." Menzies sat back and in the rear-view mirror I could see him concentrating until he put it together. "Tony Aardehuis. Did your independent study on *A Man For All Seasons.*"

"That's right."

He was quiet for a few kilometres while we drove back towards Armagh. Then he said, "What a return on time invested. Train them up and they come back to rummage through your drawers."

"Just doing my job."

He snorted, then grimaced at a pain he seemed to hold under his shirt with a single hand. "That's what the common man said. You remember the common man?"

"Turns into the executioner," I said. But this was no time for a literary discussion. Quiet filled the little car and for once even Howard seemed loaded with silence. I don't know what the others were thinking but my mind was pulled too many ways; wanting Howard free and clear of this mess, looking for a way that a guy I'd once liked could possibly be innocent, seven years as a cop settling on me with the sad truth that evidence rarely lies.

Then Menzies asked, "Is Ryan Boyd still at home?"

In the rear-view mirror our eyes met. He knew I wouldn't say, but he looked for an answer anyway, tired brown eyes searching until I flicked them off. He'd been ordered by the court to have no contact with the boy. Why did he want to know?

But he didn't stop.

"Ryan has a sister. About six years old. She broke her arm about a week ago. Is she still at home?"

Only a few minutes later Menzies doubled over, quiet with it at first, until the nausea kicked in and he started to heave, empty and sweat faced, against the window. At Emergency the stone-faced nurses admitted the accused sexual exploiter right away. They even found him a private room.

• • •

"This picturesque Ontario town was, until the arrest of Joseph Menzies, known primarily for its historic buildings and prize-winning dairy herds."

The reporter stood in front of our picturesque post office holding a microphone like an ice cream cone, talking to the huge camera as if none of the onlookers, kids on their lunch hour, folk trying to get their mail without tripping on the cables, existed.

"But residents of Armagh have been shaken by news that a 20-year veteran teacher on the staff of Armagh Collegiate Institute has been charged with sexual exploitation and the manufacture of child pornography. School officials, while declining to comment on the case, have suspended the accused with pay pending the outcome of the trial. Following his release on bail yesterday, Menzies was admitted to local hospital suffering from stress related symptoms."

"I'd give the bastard some stress," said a quiet voice next to me. Stan Scott, still in his postie shorts with a slack mail bag across his chest, shook his head while contemplating a parent's worst nightmare.

"Your girls old enough for high school?" I asked.

"Next year." Stan's smile was a twitch of pride escaping the present horror. "Thank God you got him now."

The reporter moved into the crowd, trawling for the perfect sound bite, snagging the occasional catch:

"It's terrible. Just terrible. A teacher. Who can you trust anymore? Ought never to be let out, these people. Once you get 'em you got to keep 'm behind bars. The laws is way too soft. I always thought he was a little strange. Like, you know, different?"

He approached a clutch of lanky high school boys who watched sombrely, hands shoved deep into the pockets of their baggy pants, but for some reason they backed away, an odd response, I thought, from that media savvy generation.

But they shook their heads "no" most definitely, like colts puzzled by a new feed or a strange run of fence line. The tallest colt of all was my nephew Jonas.

Looking at Jonas is seeing myself at fourteen: already six foot, not an extra ounce on his loose bones, tanned face under dirty blond hair and the long Aardehuis nose shaping up nicely. I was pleased he came over as soon as he saw me, cop uncle apparently still acceptable; snake oil reporter clearly not.

"What a bunch of jerks," he said, tipping his head toward the cluster of reporters and camera men.

"What's bugging you?"

We moved out of the crowd and crossed the street.

Forehead wearing a deep crease, he looked at me and said, "They're saying it was Ryan Boyd." A statement, not a question. Full marks for accuracy to the small town pipeline.

"I can't talk about it, Jonas. Sorry."

"I know. But that's what they're saying." His ears pinked up with embarrassment and the burden of trying to get out what he needed to say, and suddenly I was worried about what that could be. Surely my brother's boy had played no part in that story? Surely.

I said, "You got time for lunch?"

We drove up the road to the **Two x Four Diner** where he reassured his uncle by downing a bowl of chili, rolls, a milkshake. Could a boy who'd been drawn into ring of pornographers and paedophiles eat like that? Only when he wiped the sugar of two doughnuts from his chin did I ask, "How did you know it was Ryan Boyd?"

He blushed again. "It's around. And about Mr. Menzies. They're saying he was, you know, pictures and stuff? With Ryan?"

His long fingers twisted the napkin; his eyes met mine and left. He wasn't enjoying this. So why talk about it?

"Hypothetically." I said.

"I'm in Mr. Menzies' class. Ryan sits beside me."

"Yeah?"

"The thing is, if anyone asked who was hitting on who, I would have said it was Ryan after Mr. Menzies."

"Why?"

"He kept hanging around after class. Mr. Menzies would keep someone else behind too. Hang around to discuss an assignment or something. He made me go over an essay that was already marked. Like he didn't want to be alone with Ryan."

"Did Menzies ever say that?"

Jonas shook his head. "It was just a feeling. But why else would Ryan do that picture in the washroom?"

"What?"

His eyes widened with surprise. "You didn't know? Three days ago, Wednesday maybe, there was this drawing on the wall in the boy's can. Permanent black marker, 150 centemetres high. Kind of a cartoon of Mr. Menzies. Gross. They never caught anyone, but it was Ryan, for sure. He was always doodling in his books. Did these weird triangle eyes."

Jonas looked closely at me, checking his progress. "The thing is, he was trying to get Mr. Menzies. Not the other way around."

I stirred my coffee, trying to see what it changed. "Abuse victims act strange sometimes, Jonas. Try to feel better by pretending it's a good thing."

But he shook his head, stubborn and frowning. "No way. Mr. Menzies is a teacher but he's alright. Ryan Boyd is totally sick."

You and Howard MacNeill, I thought. Founding members of the Save Joe Menzies Defence League.

"I'll pass it on," I told Jonas. "You never know."

• • •

What changed if Ryan had been romancing his teacher? Nothing. Menzies was still the responsible adult. It might explain why the address had been in the email files. Mail received, not mail sent.

Then I thought back 10 years to the class I'd sat in, trying for a feel of it. For a sense of the man who'd stood at the front of the room day after day. Had I ever, under the skin, recoiled? Had I had the smarts to do it? And how could the world be so different, so soon, for Jonas, who sighted who was hitting on who like he was watching *The Price is Right?*

Back at the detachment Rob told me about the man who'd phoned again and again to report that eggs were being thrown at Menzies' house. "He said: 'I don't care what they do to the pervert's place but they're trampling on my flowers'."

Sergeant Carr laughed, and added, "Then we got at least 10 calls telling us where to look for other suspects. Someone even suggested the old guy in the nursing home who's always squeezing the nurses." Then he stopped laughing and said, "Seriously, though. I want to look at all Menzies' known associates. That back porch drop box has to have other users. Like maybe that guy who runs the hardware. He belongs to some history club with Menzies, and he bailed him too."

Carr looked at me, his face saying, "Don't I always say you shouldn't work your hometown?" His mouth saying, "You think?"

I felt my neck turn red with anger, thinking this was how Howard had felt. "I know the guy. It has to count for something."

"No way."

"That's what they always say." said Carr, "Right? I can't believe it. I can't believe it, and then finally they have to believe."

"The thing is," I said, trying to look neutral, uninvolved. "You got to make sure it doesn't turn into a witch hunt."

The next caller was Howard's shop assistant, saying a rock had just sailed through the window at MacNeill's Hardware.

A few hours later at the end of my shift I went up to the hospital and gave Howard his current popularity rating. He just shrugged, more preoccupied with the still figure on the bed, and his eyes were sombre with worry and a bitterness I'd never seen there before.

"He's getting worse. So maybe he'll die and save the taxpayers the cost of prosecution."

"Doesn't he have any family to come and sit with him?"

"One sister in Calgary."

I stepped over to the windowsill to check out the flowers the patient had been sent, surprised he'd got any. In fact, there were three. A bunch of white carnations in a jam jar signed "OAC English". Two florist arrangements, one from the English Department. The other unsigned. Just a cartoon figure waving hello from the tiny card. A cartoon character with bandy legs, top hat, toothy smile. And a pair of triangle eyes.

I went right back to the detachment but before I had time to find him Sergeant Carr stuck his head out and called me into his office. "An anonymous call just came in, from a phone booth in Kingston. I think it was from a teacher at the school."

He passed across a scribbled note:

"Ryan Boyd sent emails to Joe Menzies soliciting a sexual relationship. The administration has them all on file."

"Why the cloak-and-dagger? Why not just tell us?"

"All that stuff's confidential, maybe. Can't look for it without a warrant, can't know it's there unless we're told."

"Now we've been told."

"Yes."

"But why wouldn't the principal tell us?"

Carr sucked hard on his moustache, drawing the upper lip down in thought. "The guy's new on the job. Maybe he's in over his head. Maybe there's a liability question. They're supposed to report this stuff. Guy hits a grey area, thinks too long, waits too long to report, looks bad on him. So he covers."

Then I told him what Jonas had said, how he thought Ryan had been after the teacher, about the picture on the washroom wall, the flowers on the hospital windowsill, the figure with the trademark eyes.

"What does it change?" Carr asked.

"Nothing, if Menzies took those pictures."

"Why didn't Menzies tell us Ryan was after him?"

"I don't know. It would have made sense."

Carr folded his arms and looked it over. "You mean, Ryan might have set it all up? Pictures and all? For revenge?"

I nodded. "Ryan started it and Joe wasn't interested. So he set him up."

"So why didn't the teacher talk?"

"I don't know."

Carr shrugged. It was all the same to him and maybe that's what made him a good cop. He'd apply the same focus to Ryan Boyd as he had to getting his warrant to search Menzies' house, and in the end he'd have his answer, and justice would be done. If you didn't count the the wreckage. This is what he meant, I thought, when he said you shouldn't work in your hometown.

Then he added, "You know there wasn't a single fingerprint on those pictures?"

"Like they'd been cleaned up."

He nodded. "Cleaned up. Planted? Who knows." He chewed hard on his moustache for a minute and then he said, " The teacher can't talk right now so I think we should go see this boy."

It was after 11 by the time we reached the Purcell place on the edge of town but the house lights of the shabby, unpainted bungalow were on and everyone still up, even the little girl who opened the door.

She looked about seven, long limp hair, colourless face, left arm weighted by a dirty grey cast.

No hallway. We stepped right into a living room where stale air floated on an underlay of dust, grease, and urine. The biggest piece of furniture was a hospital bed where a curled up woman, her hands twisted in on themselves, lay pointed at the television. Her eyes, dull and listless, wandered our way for a brief second, then flickered back to the screen. Off the living room a door opened and Ryan stood there with a dishtowel in his hands. The little girl went and held onto the leg of his jeans. Derek Purcell pushed himself out of a sagging armchair, hitching his pants as he came to the door, "What brings you gents out so late?" he said.

Carr is not a cop who works on instinct, and you better not accuse him of inspiration. But something flashed in the sergeant's eyes as he looked at Ryan's tense face and watched the dishtowel twist round and round in his hands.

Carr addressed himself to Purcell but his eyes were straight on Ryan, "Hi, Derek," he said, evenly. "I wanted you to hear the news before it got out."

He waited for a minute; then told them what was news to me too. "Joe Menzies died a short while ago of a heart attack."

The dishtowel stopped twisting. Ryan turned into the kitchen and I followed.

From the doorway I could hear Purcell behind me, unsure, the bluster gone from his voice like he'd forgotten his lines. "Well. That's good isn't it? I mean. For the boy? The whole thing can drop now? He won't have to talk in court?"

"I'm not sure about that," said Carr. "We have to be sure Menzies was the only one. But it looks better. Maybe the boy'll be spared appearing."

At the kitchen sink Ryan stood staring at his own reflection in the dark window. After the stale reek of the living room disinfectant assaulted my nose. The counter had been scrubbed clean, the floor gleamed. Ryan looked away from the boy in the glass, picked up a cloth and began to shine a faucet that already gleamed.

The little girl, backed into her brother as she pressed against his legs looked up at me fearfully so I squatted down on one knee and asked, "Where'd you get that big bracelet, honey?"

She froze. Looked up at her brother, big eyes pleading for advice. But Ryan was motionless, the polishing hand on the faucet still and waiting.

"It was a accident," she whispered.

"That's right!" said Purcell, from the doorway. "Fell offa the swing."

Then the little girl laughed and it was a sound I'd heard only once before, from two little girls whose laugh had a knife edge, riding in a car with a Children's Aid Society worker, and I thought, her too.

Ryan turned the faucet on full blast so you couldn't hear her next words.

"Shut that damn thing off!" said Purcell.

Ryan shut it off with a jerk. That was when he turned, face stretched into an appalling smile. It bared his teeth and made my skin crawl, so it took another second to notice that his eyes brimmed with fury and grief and guilt, and that they turned on Uncle Derek.

"She didn't fall off the swing," he whispered. "You broke her arm."

"What the hell are you saying?" The loving uncle's face flushed with anger and I took a single step into the space between him and Ryan.

"You broke her arm. And now Mr. Menzies is dead. Because you killed him."

• • •

Ten hours later we had Derek Purcell in the can and I was back at the hospital, sitting beside Howard on a chair designed for a short stay. Joe Menzies slept on, oblivious of the day or the night, the turmoil in the churning world, or the friend who sat beside him hour after hour. I sat there and told Howard what he, of all people, deserved to know.

"Purcell's been abusing the boy for years. Ryan never reported because of the sister. If he didn't go along with the uncle, the girl would get hurt. That was the threat."

Howard nodded wearily and I waited for him to tell me the cops are a bunch of idiots and we should have known better. Instead he asked, "How did Joe come into it?"

"He was good to the kid. Thought he was smart, encouraged him. But Ryan was so messed up he didn't know what to do with genuine kindness. He started fantasizing a new life with a new and better old man. Uncle Derek saw his attention straying, and set out to teach him a lesson."

"And the kid went along with it? Broke into Joe's house to take the pictures?"

"They did that one school day when they knew the house was empty." I stopped, took a deep breath. "Don't be too hard on the kid. The day before he skipped school for the photo session his little sister was casted for a broken arm. That was a warning."

Howard looked at our old teacher, a body hovering between here and there while the cords and monitors try to tether him to here.

"Why didn't Joe say anything? Why didn't he point the finger at Ryan, tell you guys about those emails?"

I didn't answer for awhile. I thought about how he'd asked in the car, driving home from the courthouse, where the children were. "Are they still at home?" he'd asked.

"Best I can figure, Joe thought it would come out in the end anyway. But Ryan and the girl were still at home. Still with Purcell. He had to wait till he was sure they'd be alright."

Then we sat for a long time beside the bed, watching the green lines track across the screen, listening in the dark to the slow rasp of struggling breath.

A Cold Spring

She showed up in town the day before my parents' 45th wedding anniversary. It was a Friday, a busy day in downtown Armagh. She wandered up and down King Street, poking in and out of stores and asking questions, and all morning the calls came in to the detachment.

The first came from my friend Howard MacNeill at the hardware store. "Hey, Tony. There was a girl in here just now, nice little looker with an Australian accent. Wanted directions out to the farm."

"I hope you gave her good ones," I said, but my heart constricted.

"A-plus," Howard went on, "So why's she looking for Mike and your dad and not for you? You need a little action, eh?"

"She say why she was here?"

"Not really. Wanted to know long your dad was in Canada and how big was the herd and how to get out there."

Howard must have heard something in my silence. "Why? What's going on?"

"She works for one of these BioTech companies. At the fair last week she was nosing around, making noises about a herd buy."

"Oh. She didn't say anything about that. You think Mike would go for it?"

Mike is my brother, my Dad's partner and future owner of the family farm. "I doubt it. But I don't want this shit right now."

Howard understood "right now". Right now was two days before the big banquet for my parent's anniversary. Right now was my Dad's third bout of radiation treatment. Right now was a bad time for a family war.

Then there was a call from the real estate broker, saying this Aussie'd been asking about property values and was there something going on he should know about. Then the postmistress, who'd given that girl with the lovely accent advice on the local motels, said didn't she look like the rest of us with that beautiful patrician nose, "You can see right away she's some relative come for your parent's party."

A nerve started to jump in my eye. Patrician nose. Who the hell was this loose cannon with the lovely accent, flailing around town with her questions? It just showed she didn't have a clue how a small town worked. Or didn't care how much damage she did.

The first time I saw her at the Royal Agricultural Winter Fair she was staring at the sign above my brother's cows like someone looking for a hidden message. In her 20s maybe, not much younger than me, and Howard was right, she could have been nice to look at. Mane of dark curly hair and that narrow thoroughbred nose. It was the relentless eyes that put you off.

Cold Spring Guernseys, read the gold letters on green, address and phone number hand-lettered by my sister-in-law: *T & M Aardehuis, Armagh, Ontario.*

"Aardehuis. What kind of name is that?" she asked.

"It's Dutch." I said, and went back to combing out a cow's tail. Most people mangled the name. She also ironed out the vowels, and sometimes her r's rolled and sometimes they disappeared.

On the other side of the cow my nephew Jonas stopped brushing down the gleaming tan and white hide to listen to her accent.

"Dutch. What part of Holland is your family from?" The name tag clipped to her Sem-OVA Australia jacket said she was Sarah Bremmer, BSc, Sales Associate, Sydney. So she was a rep for one of the international genetic firms and a person with something to sell.

"Groningen." I said.

Sarah Bremmer nodded seriously, as if this bit of trivia made all the difference. She looked at me and she looked at Jonas like she was taking face imprints. Then she looked back at the sign with that hungry look ambitious people wear.

"Cold Spring. That's a strange name for a farm."

It was a pretty feeble opening gambit for a sales pitch.

She tried again, nodding at the ribbons clipped above Cold Spring Rocket Rose (Intermediate Champion) and Cold Spring Defacto Velvet (Best Udder). "You've done very well here."

"My brother, actually. It's his farm," I said. Save the spiel for him, I meant, and went right on combing out the already silky tail hairs of our next contender. I expected Miss Sem-OVA to drop a business card and drift away but she just stood there. Looking at the cows, Jonas, and me, and the sign.

After about an hour she said, "Well. I suppose I'll drop round again."

She headed off toward the rows of Brown Swiss and Ayrshire cattle and Jonas popped up, grinning, from the other side of the cow.

"Hey, hey, Uncle Tony." I was only "uncle" when he wanted to damage my credibility. "She's goin' to drop round again." Jonas tried to mimic the accent and failed and I threw the brush at him.

After five days at the fair we were getting punchy. Tending cows in the Trade Centre is a bit like being an exhibit yourself. All day long the city people drifted past, stepping cautiously on the straw walkways to avoid trace contamination while they looked at the sheep and pigs and horses and goats. School kids straggled through and stared at the soft flanks and swollen udders of the big cows. Then they'd watch us shampoo, comb, hair spray and razor sculpt a cow's back into perfect line, and you could see in their eyes that they were trying to figure out our strange, strange life.

• • •

Not my life. I was there at the Royal only because my Dad announced at Thanksgiving, "I don't go this year to the Fair."

Too long a drive, he said, too many hours on his feet, too many nights of no sleep on a cot beside the cows.

"I'm soon 73," he said. Except he counted it zeventy sree. He didn't mention the cancer. Neither did we.

We were sitting around the turkey remains when Dad made the big announcement. It was a pass-the-torch moment, and no one knew what to say. So we said nothing. He's old, I thought. To look at as spry and wiry, his hands as hard, as ever. It was only the cancer he wore on his face, the sore on his mouth that had been cut again and again and wouldn't heal that didn't let you forget.

To Mike, my brother, it must have been bitter sweet. The end of an era. Maybe even liberation; after years of sharing the show ring he'd be walking the cows himself. But he only said, "I can't manage with just Jonas."

He was right. One man and a 15-year-old can't juggle show ring and a round-the-clock watch on the livestock.

"Take Tony," Said Dad.

And there went a week's vacation in November.

• • •

When you grow up on a farm you get used to the idea that these acres and animals are ground zero and the rest of the world is just out there. The presumption that I could or would or must drop my job when required still rankled. But that didn't stop me from enjoying the Royal. I hadn't been back since I joined the Ontario Provincial Police, and I liked watching Jonas place first in Junior Showmanship; Mike trying to be matter-of-fact about his son's win. I liked the young dairymen who talked farming as business, business, business but still showed a flicker of wonder in their eyes when a newborn calf slid out of his mother and landed in the straw.

And I liked the old guys who came around to ask after my dad.

Some had been show ring rivals for years. Some were Dutch immigrants like him who met every year to play scrabble in the hotel and swap stories about the old country.

"I can't believe Teunis didn't come dis year," they'd say, slipping in and out of Dutch like fish flipping from fresh to salt water and back again.

"You got your *vader*'s nose. You're de young Teunis?"

"Tony."

"De policeman?"

"That's right."

"Zo, zo. Your father didn't come this year. Ik can niet believe it." The old guy's wispy white hair stood out around a pink face that wagged from side to side, sceptical that arthritis alone could keep any man away from the Royal Winter Fair. "Teunis Aardehuis. I can't believe he's getting old. Shust so hard as myself. He was en wilde yong man, *weet je wel?*"

My father, a wild boy in his younger days. I must have looked sceptical. His eyes crinkled at the corners and he shook his head at the arrogance of the young.

"We waar boys together, you know. He was busy with the girls in those days. There was one pretty *meisje* we were both chasing. And the war. You never knew your *vader* if he didn't tell you some stories about the war."

"A few," I admitted.

In fact, as a kid I'd begged for those spine-shiver tales. Radios hidden under floor boards. Messages passed hand to hand in the dark to people you never knew by name. I hadn't thought about my dad's war stories in years but, standing there breathing in the rich barn smell of purebred cattle, the feelings came right back: delicious fear, and the deep conviction that my dad, My Dad, had been one of the good guys.

"You knew him back then?"

"Hij was van de next village."

Then Mike called for help with the grooming. I meant to get back to the old guy and pick up some teasing material to bother my dad with, but I didn't cross his path again.

The Fair was like that. Business contacts forged in the aisles of the Semen and Embryo dealers, quaint agricultural products like the Cozy-Cow Mattress System; acquaintances picked up and dropped again every November. They came and went; easily known, easily forgotten.

I would have felt the same about the Australian woman, except that Jonas and I, on the way back from dinner, spotted her watching Mike from a vantage point across an aisle of Holsteins. She was still looking at the sign, scribbling something in a notebook.

"She really likes you, Uncle Tony," said Jonas. "She's writing down your phone number."

"Nah, she's just making a mailing list so she can send out some pamphlets or something," I said. But I didn't see her write down the name and address of any other farm. When she finally turned away she struck up a conversation with the old scrabble player and more than once they looked across at Cold Spring Guernseys.

In the rush of the fair ending and loading for the long trip home I forgot her again, until Jonas, in the dark cab of the pickup asked, "So, how did the farm get that name anyway?"

"What?" said Mike, taking his eyes off the road for a minute.

"There was this Australian woman at the Fair."

"Yeah, I talked to her," said Mike. "She was fishing for a contract I think, but I really couldn't make her out and didn't have the time to try."

"She said Cold Spring Farm was a strange name. And it is, when you come to think about it. So how come you named it that?" asked Jonas.

"Not me," said Mike, who is quiet and smart and doesn't have a poetic bit of cartilage in his body.

"Maybe it's always been that way," I suggested. "Since before Dad bought the place."

"Nah," Mike said, like he was pulling memories from the back of his brain. "The stock that came with the place were registered different. I've seen it in the records. So Dad must have picked it." He half smiled at Jonas. "Come to think of it, it is kind of weird. Everyone else has Sunnydale or Bonnybrae or like that painted on the barn. We get Cold Spring. Might as well call it Slow Start Farm."

"Bad Weather Farm," suggested Jonas.

"Wet Winter," I offered.

"Cloudy Sky"

"Frozen Fields."

That took care of a few miles and then Jonas said, "I still don't know why Opa called it Cold Spring Farm."

Mike stared over the steering wheel at the black ribbon of 401 East we'd be following all the way home. "Maybe it was a cold spring the year he bought the place. Or maybe he meant the creek."

"I'll ask him," said Jonas.

It was one in the morning when we finally drove down the lane. The light was still on in my father's house and before we had the back of the trailer open his wiry, slightly stooped shadow emerged out of the dark to help us unload the champions.

"*Goed gedaan*," he said when he saw the ribbons, and expressed his feelings by giving Jonas' spiked hair a dressing down.

Then, with morning milking and my dayshift just hours away, we put the cows in the barn and I drove back to town. The Royal Winter Fair, a woman from Australia, and the name under which a herd of cows were registered just left my head.

The next day was one of those grey November troughs between the colour of fall and first snow. A slate grey sky hung above the town like a roof about to fall and by midafternoon the streetlights had come on. Covering the front desk, I had to stifle a yawn when the phone rang.

"OPP Armagh."

"Sheldon Gottlieb, QC. Law firm of Gottlieb, Rice & McMahan." A port wine voice. Assured. A little pompous.

"How can I help you?"

Slight hesitation. "Sorry to use your services to such a mundane end. I tried the post office but they're leaving the populace at the mercy of an answering machine. Can't get a real human being at all. The thing is, I'm meeting a client there on Saturday; we'll be calling on one of your local families, and these country addresses are a little obscure. RR 2. Can you translate that into road directions?"

"What's the name, sir?"

"There's another puzzle …" He started to spell. "A A R D E …"

"Aardehuis."

"Is *that* how it's said!"

"I'm sure that's how you say it."

"They have a place called Cold Spring Farm?"

The temperature in the room seemed to drop. I said, "That family's located on the north side of Highway Two, west of the village of Kerry. You cross a set of railroad tracks, then a bridge over King's Creek. After that it's the first farm on the right."

"Excellent. I won't go wrong now. And, just one other … I've had no dealings with these people before." The voice turned sweet, coaxing. "One doesn't like to walk unawares into a hornet's nest, so to speak. There wouldn't be any little difficulty I should be aware of?"

"None at all," I said. "Upstanding local family."

Thank you very much, officer …"

"Constable." My eyes landed on the nameplate on the empty desk beside me. "Constable Robson."

Wide awake now, I called a friend from university, Martin Malley, who'd stayed there long enough to come out a lawyer. An hour later he called back to tell me that Sheldon Gottlieb's firm specialized in family law.

Family law? Family law meant parents and children. Adoptions. Divorces. Custody.

"They have a place called Cold Spring Farm."

Only one person had ever paid attention to that name. Her name was Sarah something-or-other from Australia. She worked for a Biotech firm. She made a big deal of the name of the farm. And what had I told her? We were Dutch, from Groningen. That my Dad came to Canada after the war. I'd seen her pumping one of his old cronies.

For a long time I ignored the papers on my desk, looking out the window at the threatening sky, wondering how Australia connected with the north of Holland connected with a farm in Armagh and a lawyer with a family law brief in his pocket.

And I thought about family. How most of the time we fool ourselves that we've got that whole thing figured out. Brothers and sisters neatly labelled: The smart one. The hard worker. The rebel.

And parents. The farmer and his wife. Hardworking. Clean living. Loving couple.

But what did I know for sure? My dad came to Canada in '49, a 23-year-old immigrant kid on his own, working mines and lumber mills until he met mom at a Dutch Club dance, married and went back to the dairy business that beat in his blood. But my parents had a past I knew nothing about. The only colour I could give it was the blue of the aerograms that filled the mailbox at the end of the lane, and the only history I knew were the bits they chose to tell. No village of relatives, neighbours, old school mates to fill in the gaps.

I thought about young people growing up in a war when it must have felt like nothing would ever be normal again. About an old guy saying, "In those days he was always busy with the girls."

Dinner that night was at Mike's place, a celebration of our show ring triumphs and a last round of preparations for the anniversary banquet. My parents walked over from their house, the bungalow Mike built for them in the old apple orchard when he got married. We ate a roast from one of the grainfed calves and vegetables from my sister-in-law's garden. Dad put us through a full debriefing of the fair. My mother and Shelley, my sister-in-law, wrestled with the road map of the banquet hall. For dessert we ate Mom's almond cake, and when she set it and a coffee in front of me she said, "You're so quiet, Tony. Still missing sleep?"

"I guess," I said.

My mother is one of those tall, quiet women you find in the back row of the group picture, the lady with straight back and soft grey hair and eyes that look happy with the world. I was born when she was forty, separated from Mike and my sister by a decade. *Onze nakomertje*, she called me. The latecomer. More than once when I was a kid she'd been mistaken for my grandmother. Then her eyes would wrinkle into an even deeper smile and I'd think, how stupid can you get? Couldn't they tell she was one of the youngest people in the world?

She was still young, and independent too. Every year she went back to Holland on her own because my father refused to go back even for a visit.

But that was my mother, she was herself and she left others a space to be.

Over coffee I told dad about the old farmers who'd missed him. About the one who said he'd been a wild one for the girls. I tried to make it sound teasing, "I got the idea you got the girl he wanted."

"Ja, she was a very nice girl," Dad said. "She had dark curly hair and cheeks like apples, and you know, I can see her face, but I can't remember her name?"

He shook his head at the unpredictable brain. Mike's Stephie, who is eight and just the age to be curious without caution, asked, "So why didn't you marry her, Opa?"

"Ach, *kind*," he laughed, looking at my mother across the table, "I knew there was a girl who'd be getting on a boat for Canada so I could meet her at a dance on the other side of the world."

"And that was Oma!" said Stephie. But then she looked puzzled again. "But wasn't the apple girl sad when you didn't pick her?"

"I don't know," said my father, the teasing gone. "It was the war. She was only visiting there for awhile because it wasn't safe in Rotterdam for the bombing. She went home before the bad winter of '45. A good thing for her, because in the north we were still starving with the Germans and the south was already free. But I never saw her again."

"That's so sad!" said Stephie.

Sad was how I felt, sitting there doing the math, spinning scenarios. Eighteen when the war ended. Old enough to have fathered a child by a woman who might immigrate to Australia. Enough decades past for that child to have a daughter who'd grow up and bump into us at the Royal Winter Fair. Somehow the Cold Spring name had made her stop and look at us. Who knew what that was about. A song, maybe? A poem?

I didn't blame him for being young once, but I minded for my mother. How could he stick the words from an old love on the side of our barn?

· · ·

And then she showed up in town and set the detachment phone ringing. I made some calls of my own and found out she was staying at the Upper Canada Motel on the beach road. The same hotel where we'd eat tomorrow night with a hundred people gathered to celebrate a long marriage. Hannah, on the desk said, "I didn't give her one of the rooms you reserved. Sorry. I kinda wondered if she was one of your people, but she didn't say ... Nice accent, eh? Nice of her to come so far. She a cousin or something?"

"Or something."

The last phone call came from Martin Malley in Ottawa with more intelligence on the life and times of Sheldon Gottlieb, QC.

"Hey, Tony! I got some more info on your Gottlieb guy," said Martin, all cheerful and proud of himself, "Turns out he does tons of *pro bono* for The Simon Wiesenthal Centre. He was on the team that got that death camp guy deported."

He paused, waiting for the congratulations. And waited.

"That any help to you, Tony?"

"Yeah. Yeah, it is."

Another long pause. "What's going on, Tony?"

"I don't know. I just don't know."

When you don't know you're stuck with the few bits you have, and the bits swirled and spun in front of me. My Dad, a young man in an occupied country. A family lawyer. Or a war crimes lawyer? A woman from the other side of the world who'd picked us out of the lineup at the Royal Winter Fair.

Saturday, the lawyer had said. Tomorrow.

At the best, a surprise granddaughter. At the worst, an avenging angel. I remembered reading in the paper about the man who got deported, and how fleetingly I'd pitied a family that could be so duped, so long.

Mike. Should I tell him? It would all matter more to him. He'd worked along side, earned the acres, stepped into shoes that had walked places we knew nothing about. The only thing that would gain, I thought, was one more person to hang high on a roof about to fall, hoping for the best and sick with dread.

So what I did was go home after my shift, sleep restlessly, and in the morning park myself in the yard of Brady's John Deere Sales and Service, across the street from the Upper Canada Motel.

He'll be driving a Buick Regal, I thought. He'll get here about eleven if he leaves Toronto at seven. He'll be wearing a light camel hair coat and carrying a soft leather case.

Peter Brady arrived to open the dealership doors, gave me a half wave and ignored me after he saw I was watching the motel. A few guests piled their luggage into trunks and drove off. Motel staff pushed their big linen carts from room to room, getting ready for the next round which would include arrivals for my parent's anniversary.

I was only right about the time. At 11:21 a burgundy Lincoln pulled up in front of Room 9. Sheldon Gottlieb looked about 60, bald with round horn rimmed glasses, and he wore a short brown leather jacket. He left his case in the car.

He knocked. Sarah Bremmer came out right away and climbed into his car. I followed them down the beach road and back through town. Down six miles of highway two, west. Through the village of Kerry. Across the CN tracks. Over King's Creek bridge.

They turned down the first farm lane on the right, and I kept right on going. It took five minutes to reach the next driveway and pull up. I sat there thinking I could just go back to town and act surprised like everyone else when the explosion blew. Or I could go on and just drive the straight road out of sight. It was my mother that made me turn back. When I did, suddenly it felt so urgent, to be there, buffer whatever was coming and of course, a combine filled most of the road and I had to crawl back behind him.

Jonas was heading from house to barn as I spit past on the gravel lane and turned down my parent's drive. I parked beside the Lincoln, took the steps two at a time, stepped through the kitchen and stopped in the living room doorway.

There they were, sitting with coffee cups and spice cookies in their hands and I hadn't missed the blast. My mother sat as upright as ever, my father looked at Sheldon Gottlieb and Sarah Bremmer with sharp eyes and the wisp of smile he wore at the sales barn, waiting for the right moment to bid. He was enjoying himself.

"My son," he said, introducing me to Sarah Bremmer.

She gave me the briefest nod of recognition. Then she turned back to my father, and what she was doing was weighing, measuring, judging. And my father looked back at her, like he was waiting for the moment to bid.

Sheldon Gottlieb launched into a run on sentence about the work of his Centre which was "… very diverse, and at the present time engaged in international inquiries on several fronts which you can appreciate are matters very delicate and we try to be as discreet and respectful of the privacy of our contacts as possible …"

My mother did most of the listening. The girl and my father looked and weighed.

"… perhaps you've heard about the effort to restore confiscated property to the rightful owners from who it was stolen by the Nazis and their collaborators …"

My father's brow furrowed, like the bidding had gone wrong. Distracted, he reached across for the sugar pot, dumped one, two scoops into his cup.

"It's been a bitter winter," Sarah Bremmer said. To my father.

In Australia?

Sheldon Gottlieb stopped dead. My father swung round to look at her and for a second he had a young man's face, and then sugar landed in a splash on the dark red carpet.

"And a cold spring coming." he said, staring hard at her.

"But that will make the tulips last longer." She bit so hard on her lips they turned white, holding in whatever it was. Rage? Euphoria? She couldn't help but lean forward.

"I think you might have something for me," she said quietly.

"Ja. I do." My father got up and went into the bedroom.

Silence waited for him. I shifted to sit beside my mother.

She didn't seem surprised when my father returned carrying a carved box. From it he took old passports and other, yellowed, documents and set them on one side. Then, from the bottom, he lifted a small brown parcel and passed it to the girl.

She unfolded the brittle paper carefully. Lifted up a signet ring with red stone. A silver pocket watch. A handful of photographs. Black and white, odd sizes, and she spread them one by one across her lap, looking down with the dark hair hiding her eyes.

"Is this what you expected to find?" Sheldon Gottlieb asked.

He meant, "Is anything missing?"

She looked up at him, uncertain, as if it took a minute to remember who he was. "These are the only pictures we have."

He tried again. "But weren't you told the family fortune should be here?"

"Not in those words." she said. Like she was reluctant to be anything but glad, and I decided that I liked Sarah Bremmer after all.

"But it is," said my father. He reached across, took the watch from her hands and opened the case. "There are numbers scratched here."

Whump of footsteps on the porch, the backdoor opened, closed. Two pairs of boots thumped on the mat and Jonas and Mike appeared in the doorway.

"A serial number?" said Sheldon Gottlieb.

"I thought so too," said my Dad. "For a long time. But I think now they must be for something else. I might be wrong but I think this is an account number. For a bank. Perhaps in ..."

"... Switzerland," finished the lawyer.

They say when a tornado passes by it leaves an energy behind. The air crackles with it, twangs like the string of a violin.

Mike said, "What the hell's going on?"

We had to stand up and move. Sarah went to my father and took his hand in both of hers. I introduced Mike and Jonas to Mr. Gottlieb and my mother poured more coffee. When standing started to feel just as desperate we sat down again and my father explained how the brown parcel had come to him.

"1945. Winter. The winter with long teeth, they called it. The south of Holland had been liberated but in the north we were still under the thumb. Bitter cold and whatever food the Germans could find they took and shipped it out. A strange time because on the one hand everyone knew the nightmare would be over soon, and on the other the occupiers were harsher than they'd ever been. Starving people begged from farm to farm. Nazi sympathizers knew their time was running out.

"I was 18. Only 13 when the war started. I delivered messages for my uncle Willem, and packets that must have been ration books — always best not to know. He tried to keep me in the background, away from sabotage. Away from the human cargo of Jews and underground men on the run.

"But that winter he ran out of choices. In February he came and asked me to go at night to meet a man at the *kerkhof*. Because of the curfew I came there over the field paths and found him crouched behind my great-grandfather's stone at the back of the churchyard. A young fellow, maybe 20 years. Terrible cold and he had only a thin coat but he held his white face up to the moon like a man who's been indoors for too long. We exchanged these sign words about the winter and the cold spring and the *tulpen* that would last longer. Then I took him, again over the fields, to the man who drove the milk tanker from farm to farm. All night we hid in the barn. He'd been hidden with an old spinster woman now fallen ill so a new place had to be found for him in a hurry. In two years I was the first person he'd talked to besides the old woman and it was too cold to sleep. He talked all night."

My father stopped, like he could still hear the far off murmur of that voice.

"Before the sun came up we climbed into the tank of the milk truck and drove north towards the coast. At two more farms we stopped and more people climbed into the belly of the tank and then we could feel we were bumping down a rough lane and then he and I were dropped at the edge of the forest. From there I was to guide him into the bush to a *jachthut*, a hunter's cabin deep in the woods. That's where it all went wrong."

His words moved faster over this part of the story, the lines deepened in his face.

"We didn't know the groundskeeper had been caught and replaced with a collaborator. I should have known there was something wrong when I smelled the smoke coming from the hut fire. Common sense would say there would be no fire to alert the authorities but I had never been there before and didn't know the routine. And there is still part of you that just thinks it's cold and the smell of a fire on a winter night is a welcome thing.

"They must have heard us coming. We were very near before we realized. Then they were after us and we decided to split up. I took a handful of dirt and smeared it on his white face so it wouldn't show in the dark and that was when he gave me the little bundle.

"If they catch us you are more likely to live," he said. "This is all that I have for my family. Save it for them if you can."

"Then he disappeared into the dark. A few minutes later I heard yells of triumph that he was caught. I was luckier. Maybe they thought there was only one of us. I managed to crawl away and make it home. It took me three days to do it, but I finally made it home."

His eyes were bleak as he looked at Sarah and asked, "He was your grandfather?"

"No, my grandfather's brother. They took him to Westerbork and he met my grandfather there. Before he died he told him about this Dutch boy in Groningen to whom he'd given the parcel." She smiled a little sheepishly, "He said he had a big nose, and repeated the passwords they'd exchanged. That was all we ever knew. My father learned it from his father and he drilled it into us. "A bitter winter. A cold spring coming. But that will make the tulips last." I always thought it was more of a ritual of memory than anything else. I never thought it would connect with you."

Dad said, "You know, I put that in the newspaper many times before I left Holland, and I always had the feeling someone would come." He grinned. "But I was beginning to give up hope."

Mike said, "I never heard about this Uncle Willem."

"He was shot two weeks later."

Sheldon Gottlieb, QC, drove back to Toronto. Sarah stayed for the anniversary banquet where I introduced her as an old friend of the family. It was a nice party, a good meal followed by a video history of my parents lives that made no mention of dark rides in the empty belly of a milk truck or gunshots in the cold spring. And then there was dancing.

About midnight my father disappeared and my mother sent me to find him in time to say goodbye to guests who were starting to look for their coats. I found him at the edge of the parking lot, a cigarette hanging from the wrong corner of his mouth.

"Don't tell your mother," he said. "What does one more matter?"

I nodded, and then we stood looking at the night November sky. I was taller than him to start with, and he looked small, shrunken in the folds of his new suit and finally I said what I had to say.

"I'm sorry, Dad."

"Vor what?"

"I knew that lawyer was coming. I kind of got the wrong idea about what he might have been after ..."

Dad nodded, cut me off. "It's okay. Now you know why I could never go back. It's a terrible thing, not knowing who you really know, who you can trust. I had to get out of there."

Bare branches crackled in the cold wind and we stood there long enough for him to grin at me and light up another smoke.

I said, "She's going to smell it anyway."

"I know," said one of the good guys.

The Robbie Burns Revival

"A cop should have a wife to keep him sane."

This was article two in Sergeant Carr's drill book. The first was that a police officer should never work where he grew up. My first day posted back to Armagh he said, "You hometown boys got all these old loyalties and no judgement. A cop should be on the outside."

Carr was so far on the outside he drove 30 miles every week to play cards with the guys in the next detachment. His idea of a friend for his wife was another cop's wife. For one tense week his idea of a date for me was his sister — Eastern Ontario Women's Bowling Champion. It took a pair of tickets to the Kingston Opera, lent by my friend Howard MacNeill, to get off that hook. After four seemingly endless hours of Wagner I was a free man again.

For the first six months Carr scrutinized every move I made. "You go to school with this guy?" he'd ask about a parking ticket. "Any history I need to know about?" when he sent me out with a summons.

But all that stopped after the death of Matt Molloy. Even Carr knew we'd have charged the wrong person with murder if I hadn't grown up in Armagh.

For starters, I would never have been there when it happened if I hadn't been Howard MacNeill's buddy since high school. Or if he hadn't come up with the idea of a Burns Night to break the boredom of January. And if he hadn't exacted payment for his Wagner tickets by insisting I be there.

"I'm not Scottish," I said when he invited me. I'd stopped into his hardware store to restock the cruiser with Kleenex and flashlight batteries and found myself trying hard to duck a party that sounded like a cross between the Highland Games and pub night with the poets.

"It's Aardehuis, not MacDonald. Remember?"

"All cultures are united by great art," said Howard, and his big arm magnanimously waved away any obstacle posed by my genetic material. My Dutch parents had given me the 183 centimetres plus, the grey eyes and ash blond hair of north Holland, but no escape clause for Burns Night.

"And the new teacher will be there. You seen her yet? I told her all about you."

Yes, I had met the new woman in town. I didn't bother to tell Howard our first encounter had been less than heaven. Her the teacher supervisor at the Armagh Collegiate Christmas dance. Me giving her hell while I tried to keep a drunk kid from drowning himself in the toilet.

"You'll love it," said Howard, grinning at me across the counter, his eyes gleaming with a fervour I recognized from old experience. "Haggis, the finest ales and whiskys, and the poems of the immortal Robert Burns."

"What the hell is haggis?"

"Haggis is spiced guts boiled with oatmeal in a sheep stomach."

"I can't wait."

"Just remember the Bowling Queen."

Thankfully, the bell above the door rang and in came Matt Molloy and his wife Helen and a blast of January. They stomped the snow off their boots and Howard came around the counter to show them the snow blower he'd set aside for them. I would have made my escape right then if I had paid for my stuff.

Instead, I made small talk with Helen while Howard and Matt circled the snow blower like priests around an altar.

The Molloys are what get called in Armagh, "a nice couple". In their fifties, they'd retired to set up a bed and breakfast on the beach road. The nice couple had never had any children to annoy the neighbours. And, though Matt had a slight rep for stroking young ladies and a passion for gambling, they never fought in public or drank at separate tables in the Rose and Thistle. So they were a nice couple.

"What are the odds of this thing lasting out the winter?" said Matt, "In case I kick off and Helen has to do it on her own?" In his former life he'd been an insurance salesman and I could remember him talking odds and chances across my father's kitchen table, trying to sell house insurance, car insurance, making a case for crop insurance in the days when it was still a novelty. Always that phrase "odds are good that you'll need this policy one year in ten … odds are 99 to one you'll never need this coverage. You just don't want to be in the one …"

I think my Dad got his insurance from Harry Desmond.

"Stop it, Matt." Helen turned away, a cross look on her face. "Stop talking about kicking off."

I said to Helen, "I thought you two went south every winter? You can't have many guests this time of year."

"No. We just have that new teacher and she'd be fine on her own. One of the family by now."

Helen had high cheek bones and clear blue eyes that paid attention when you talked. She was still an attractive woman in a Nordic, healthy kind of way. "Matt had a heart attack in August." The lines around her mouth turned down and she aged a decade. "Now he won't go. Not Florida. Not even the reserve casino."

"Sorry to hear it. Not fit to travel?"

"No. It's all under control. They got him on those beta blockers."

Beta Blockers. There was a guy at my first posting, way back in Port Rose, on those things. Willis had the same heart attack gut that circled Matt's middle and I'd listened to a few long moans about the side effects. "So I'm still alive but, you know, you got no interest. Lucky me, one of the percent with the side effects. You know what I'm saying? You kinda miss it and you kinda don't, cuz you got no interest."

Helen sounded sad and discouraged and I thought of my 70-year-old mother going to Holland every year on her own because my dad was too stubborn to leave the farm. "So, go by yourself, Helen," I said, "Or with a friend."

Matt's head reared up from the other side of the machine like he'd heard a thunderclap in the distance. "Hey!" he said, "Who'd make me that perfect cup of coffee?"

Helen looked at me like I'd spoken a foreign language. "Oh? I couldn't leave him on his own!"

It was an odd feeling, like bumping into an invisible barrier. Soft, but impermeable, like plastic wrap. If that's marriage, I thought, you could suffocate in there. Especially with a guy who had no interest.

"So that's why you need the snow blower. The heart attack."

She nodded, looking at Matt where his grey head bent beside Howard, pondering the 10-horsepower, 28-inch, electric start, two-stage marvel on the floor.

"Odd man," she said. "Won't go south because he has to die at home, but do you think I could convince him to let me take care of the driveway? Says he wants to die on the job." Her smile was wry, like she partly admired his artful dodges, partly like she was looking at defeat.

Then the bell rang again and in came Dan LeBlanc, just finished his school bus route. He started roaring when he saw the snow blower. "My machine! Hell, MacNeill, you could 'a called to tell me it was in!"

Matt looked at Howard. Howard looked at Dan and said, "Sorry Dan, this one's Matt's. Your machine is still on back order, sad to say."

I hoped I was the only who noticed the half inch of red creeping up the back of Howard's neck, the only one who could track the train of thought: Matt Molloy had a heart attack; bump him up to the top of the orders. That'd be Howard.

It was just bad luck he had to be caught in the act by Dan LeBlanc.

Now, if Sergeant Carr were watching he'd think it was just about a snow blower. He'd have no idea that five years ago Dan and Matt fell out over a pile of rubble dumped over a fence, an epic engagement including by-law officers, a comic column in the local paper and 99 versions of who had said what to who.

Carr would think the two of them were staring at Howard because they wanted him to solve the problem, not because they still hadn't figured out how to talk to each other.

Howard said, "There's an upgrade on sale, Dan. Eleven-horse, 30-inch width. I couldn't reach you right away so I took a gamble. I thought with your yard you'd need the wider cut. They said it would be here Friday."

Dan looked at the machine. "This one's assembled."

"I'll take care of yours too," said Howard.

So Dan nodded and the deal was clinched. There might even have been a twinge of relief in that nod, like he was just as glad not to have a fight about it. "Just so long's it's here before the weekend. Radio says there's a big storm coming."

He turned stiffly toward the door, but Howard stopped him. "What are you reading at Burns Night?"

" 'Ah For Honest Poverty'," said Dan, with a slight emphasis on "honest".

"One of my favourites," said Matt, glaring at his back as the door shut behind him.

"There you go," said Howard, coming over to ring up my stuff. He could afford to leave Matt alone with the machine now that he'd defended his right to it. "There you go, culture as the healer of ancient wounds."

"Aren't you afraid he'll want the upgrade too?"

"He'll have enough trouble shoving that thing around," said Howard.

He threw my purchases into a paper bag, then reached back and added a paperback from a stack on the shelf: *The Collected Poems of Robert Burns.*

"Pick one of these and be ready to stand up and read." He grinned. "Matt and Helen are coming. Right?"

"Right," said Matt, looking up from his new love.

I said, "What do you mean, I got to stand up and read a poem?"

"Alright, maybe we'll let you sit. Or you can sing if you like. I'll lend you my CD of Burns songs."

"Oh great, I'll get right on that."

I took the bag and my change and headed for the door, but Howard didn't let up. "We need the humanizing influence of the arts in this community, especially those engaged in the demoralizing trade of law enforcement. In the depths of January, the post Christmas lowering of spirits, we need to encounter the spirit of true art ..."

"You mean spirits," I said.

"Hear, hear!" said Matt, who would be dead in a few days.

The door closed behind me.

I threw the Kleenex and batteries across the front seat and started up the OPP cruiser to get the heat going but didn't pull out into the street right away. Downtown Armagh, all two blocks of it, huddled in the thin winter sun. Half the parking spaces lay buried under piles of dirty snow and only a few shoppers struggled over the icy corners, breath puffing out of their mouths in little clouds. No wonder they were in there squabbling over a snow blower. A party, for whatever reason, a room warm with a crowd of people, laughing, singing. It *was* a good idea. But a Robert Burns Night. *That* was vintage Howard MacNeill.

It's not that I have anything against poetry. I even have a degree in literature and philosophy; not a fact you advertise in the locker room.

I suppose Howard is one of those old loyalties Carr worries about. The guy you know from before your first shave. The guy you think the world would be a duller place without. I'd learned fast that the only way to handle his enthusiasms was to go with the flow and hope they'd die soon. Half the trivia cluttering my head got there by trailing him through passions that hit like successive tidal waves.

Because of Howard I play a passable collection of tin whistle tunes. I've marched in the replica uniform of the Glengarry Light Infantry Fencibles, circa 1813, hoping the gunpowder in the pan wouldn't blow off my hand. Last summer, when he caught this Scottish fever I should have known it was just a matter of time before I got sucked into the vortex.

Then again, I thought, it could be worse. How much worse? He could expect me to wear a kilt and play "Scotland The Brave" on the bagpipes.

I did owe him.

So I pulled the book of poems out of the bag, cracked it open and skimmed a few lines:

> "But oh! fell death's untimely frost,
>   That nipt my flower sae early!
> Now green's the sod, and cauld's the clay
>   That wraps my Highland Mary!"

He had to be kidding.

· · ·

Drambuie. The Glenlivet. Tartan Ale. I plunked my contribution to Burns Night, twelve bottles of MacEwan's Export, on Howard's kitchen table. Then I opened a bottle of MacEwan's for myself. From the look of the crowd I was going to need it. Outside, the forecasted storm had already dropped its first ten centimetres of huge, soporific flakes but no one seemed to have stayed home because of it.

Howard's house is a huge Victorian mansion with big rooms, wide staircases and pocket doors. Howard's parties are like family reunions that gather all the enemies in the gene pool, put a drink in their hands and wait for the explosion. If your interests ever overlapped with his you were on his guest list and, from the kitchen doorway, I surveyed the results.

Angus MacInnes, wearing a kilt, chatted with the President of the Board of Trade. Name notwithstanding, Angus is a Mohawk from Akwesasne who spends his summers in a loincloth reenacting the Six Nations contribution to the War of 1812. Board of Trade fiddles a mean "Paddy on the Turnpike". Near the fireplace the Baptist minister argued strategy at Culloden with the lonely soul who'd tried to start up a Gay Pride Day in Armagh. The snow blower rivals ignored each other from opposite corners of the room, Dan in short jacket and flaming red kilt, Matt Malloy in a suit with tartan tie holding a well-filled glass.

Would he talk to me? That afternoon Sergeant Carr had clocked him going 80 over the limit on a twist of road outside of town; surprising because Matt had never been much of a speeder. I hadn't given him the big ticket but he'd know that I knew about it, and it was just the kind of overlap Carr thought would trouble a cop in his hometown. I could hear the speech right now: "Guy gets a fine like I slapped on him from someone he's known since forever no way you're gonna sit down and have a beer together …"

I was on my way to prove him wrong when Howard grabbed my arm. "C'm'ere, I want you to meet someone."

She stood by herself in the bow window looking down at an illustrated biography of Burns, turning the pages too fast. She was slim and pretty and short, and her short dark hair looked like a lawn mower had been used for effect. For a second I wondered if she'd recognize me out of uniform. People don't always see the person writing the ticket, or giving them hell in a high school hallway.

"April Brown," said Howard, "this is Tony Aardehuis. Another Burns fan."

He smiled and waited for the click. When it didn't come, he filled the gap.

"April's the new English teacher. Filling in for Joe Menzies while he's on leave."

"Pleased to meet you," I said. We shook hands. Besides towering over her, I felt like a fool watching the secret laugh twitch behind her eyes. Brown eyes.

"Tony works for the government," said Howard.

"Oh, really. What do you do for the government?"

"I don't …"

"Statistics," said Howard. "I got to go start the piper. So take care of April, eh, Tony? She's from Toronto, she's drinking ale, and she's my resident Burns authority."

He disappeared toward the hall and as soon as he left the joke was over. I edged away so she wouldn't have to lean back to look up at me. Brown was an Anglo name, so where had she got that Latin princess look, that perfect face?

"Statistics? What was that all about?"

"Howard thinks being a cop is my social impediment."

"Is it?"

"Too soon to tell."

"So. You're a Burns fan?"

I didn't like the sarcasm in her voice. I was thinking, if we sat down I wouldn't feel like I was looming over her. Maybe I could repair the damage from our first meeting. She could explain Burns to me and I could explain how walking through puke in the boys' washroom tended to sour the mood.

"Hell, no," I said. "I'm a Howard MacNeill fan. I can't seem to say no to the guy."

She liked that and the start of a real smile opened out. "So what are you reading? One of those four line epitaphs?"

"I was thinking of "Tam o'Shanter", which is, what? Ten, 12 pages?"

"Really?"

"Well, no. Maybe eight. Pages."

She wore a cream-coloured sweater and a short knit skirt, green like late summer grass. Soft colours that moved on a body that managed to look soft and strong at the same time. "Try at once for intimacy". That was the famous poet's advice on women to his kid brother. It said so in the introduction.

Try at once for intimacy. I wondered what Miss Burns Authority thought about that.

Beside us Angus asked Dan about his tartan. Dan said his grandfather was a MacNab, descended from a guy who came to the Ottawa Valley in 1823 to escape his debts.

"Runs in the family then," said Matt Molloy, too loud, and then the pipes started up. First a hum and then a wail above the hum and then the Baptist minister piped in the haggis. Behind him came Howard and the Board of Trade guy with a little platform on their shoulders. The corpse resting on the tartan bier was a lard-coloured lump the size of a football. Someone started to clap in time to the march and the little procession carried on around the room until they stopped in front of the buffet table and set the haggis down in the centre.

Then Howard yelled, "Address 'To a Haggis'," in a voice that sounded, in the afterblast of bagpipes, like a voice on a distant radio. He stabbed the "great chieftain o' the puddin'-race", and inhaled the rising steam with an exaggerated sigh of ecstasy.

"O what a glorious sight," he intoned, "Warm-reekin', rich!"

It just goes to show you can pull off any dumb thing if you do it with enough conviction.

Then dinner. April helped Dan LeBlanc with dishing out, giving each guest a plate of taties and neeps, roast beef and of course, haggis.

Like everything else in his house Howard's dishes are bizarre. Somewhere he picked up 4,000 pieces of china that look like they come straight from a Bavarian hunting lodge, each one decorated with another kind of prey. As I came down the line I could see April looking them over, making a few swift choices about who got what plate. Helen got a doe. She gave the fox to Angus, ducks in flight to the gay guy, a stag with rampant antlers to Howard.

"Very funny," I said, as she handed me the wild boar.

Still, she walked past Howard and Angus (plotting the order in which guests would read) and Matt (hand outstretched to take the pills Helen doled out for him) to sit down beside me on the wide staircase.

We talked about where she was from (New Brunswick). Why she'd come to Armagh (first job open after she finished a stint in the Northwest Territories). How she liked the Molloy's Bed & Breakfast.

"Great," she said, but there was an edge somewhere. "They're a nice couple. But I'm looking for my own place."

"Why? It sounds perfect."

"You have your own place?"

I nodded. Three rooms over the converted feed mill with a great view of the Kerry river out the bathroom window.

"I'll swap," she said. "You can have the clean linen, daily cooked breakfast. I'll have the privacy. It'd be better for a man to live there anyway …"

She stopped, like she'd turned a corner too fast.

So not even beta blockers could keep Matt's hands to himself. She looked like she didn't want to go there so I changed the topic.

"I was a teacher," I told her. "For a year."

"So?"

"So I quit."

"Couldn't take it, eh?"

"You're right. It was way too hard. All those little weasels sticking gum into the keyboards and I couldn't arrest them."

She grinned and for some reason I wanted to go right back to the beginning and start over again.

"So about that problem at the dance …" I started.

It wasn't pipes this time, it was Howard telling us to get into the living room and prepare to do our party pieces.

If I hadn't been on edge, waiting for him to pick me to read, it would have been half enjoyable. Once in awhile a line I'd always known would jump out of a poem and I'd think, "that's Burns?" Burns had other themes, but women were his favourite. Jeannie, the wife. Also Jessie, Peggy, Nancy … The guy was either a first class alley cat or he just loved to be in love. Or maybe he was both.

When Howard gave us a break to refill our glasses April headed upstairs toward the bathroom. I fetched us both a new ale, spent a few minutes explaining to Angus why I wasn't going to be doing the Battle of Stoney Creek with them, asked Helen what she'd like (Glenmorangie, one for her and one for Matt).

"He doesn't have to go slow on the booze?" I asked. That had been another Willis moan. "One beer a day. Light beer. If you can call it beer."

"There's no managing that man," she said, looking sour. "Says he's going to live like he wants and to hell with it." And then Howard mustered us back to our places.

April still wasn't back so I went to look for her and found her cornered in the upstairs hall by good ol' Matt who'd casually occupied the whole passage with his fat self and one arm artfully draped over a bannister. She couldn't have got past him without making a scene and he was leaning in so intently he didn't hear me coming.

"Hey, Matt," I said. His hand flew off the railing and I turned him around before he knew what was happening, faced him downstairs and gave him a push in the right direction. "Helen's waiting for you."

He was smart enough to take his red face away.

"Very impressive," April said. And then, "I'm not being sarcastic."

"Is he like that all the time?"

"When he's not watching the Russian roulette scene in *The Deer Hunter* for the fortieth time. That is one weird man." Then she shrugged. "We should get down there."

While I psyched myself up for reciting "Will Ye Go to the Indies, My Mary" I thought about maybe having a quiet word with Matt who was busy trying to retrieve his dignity by picking a fight. Who knows what he said, leaning down beside the school bus driver.

Just enough to jump Dan up, shouting, "You damn liar. You've been pitching your crap over my fence for years."

Matt hurled right back, "You're so stupid you couldn't tell a fence line from a crooked furrow."

"You were born dumb and you been losing ground ever since."

"Odds are good you couldn't spell your own name."

Between us Howard and I eased the two of them, yapping like terriers and about as dangerous, to chairs on opposite sides of the room.

Helen said, "Really Howard, you think you'd know better than to put these two idiots in the same room."

Everyone looked more amused than anything else, and it would have stayed funny if Matt hadn't, the next minute, slumped sideways in his chair. Then, in slow motion, slid down to the floor.

So I never did get to read my poem.

• • •

A heart attack, pure and simple. Angus and Howard and I took turns doing CPR. Dan on the 911 line. Helen sobbing in the corner with April's arm around her. Sensible guests backed off into distant rooms, a few quietly taking themselves off home once they'd figured out there was no help to offer.

It took the ambulance a long time to get there through the heavy snow. The medics did their best, but you could tell from the first look they didn't have much hope. I drove Helen, still clinging to April's hand, to the hospital. Then, silent and sombre, we sat in the waiting room.

It took only an hour but that kind of hour is a long time. Every second feels like the years and years that might end right now, right this minute. I couldn't imagine what Helen was feeling, looking at the end of all that time together.

Once a nurse appeared and asked a lot of questions in a hurry.

"Was he exercising?

"Overexcited?

"Using a nasal decongestant?

"How much had he had to drink?"

Helen said he'd been pushing the snowblower all afternoon. That he'd been shouting at the party. And he'd been drinking. A lot. Who'd been counting?

I met April's eye and we decided not to mention he'd also been getting heated about her. Or that I might have overexcited him with a push in the right direction.

Then the hour was over and a doctor came out the swing doors and told Helen, who seemed to have run out of tears, that she'd lost her husband.

The doctor was John Byrne, the guy who'd brought me into the world when his career was still young; also Matt and Helen's family physician. He broke it to her as gently as he could, described the steps they'd taken to save him; a strategy designed, it seemed, to give her time for the first stunned realization to sink in. Then April took over and we backed off. That was when he pulled me into a corner and told me he wasn't 100 per cent happy with what had happened.

"Not what you'd expect. I don't get it. His blood pressure was way up. Shouldn't happen with the meds he was on. I can't figure it out. Not that we can understand everything. There is always that fluke."

I sometimes wonder how it would have turned out if Carr had been standing there instead of me. If he, not knowing John Byrne, would have missed the cue.

"What are you saying?"

"It just makes me a little uneasy."

Or if John Byrne, not knowing Carr, would have kept his uneasiness to himself.

I pried April away from the grieving widow long enough to ask her, "What plate did you give Matt?"

"What?"

"Never mind 'what'. I need to know what plate he ate off. Now."

There was intelligence in those eyes. I liked that. Also a stubborn streak that considered long before she finally said, "The wolf. I gave him the wolf."

I called Howard who, predictably, had not yet begun to clean up. "Find the plate with the wolf on it," I told him, "and stick it someplace safe."

Then I called Sergeant Carr and told him we had, might have, a suspicious death. That he better come and talk to the Doctor himself.

I drove Helen and April home. It was a long silent ride through the snow and you could almost feel the thoughts crackling the air. Helen adjusting to a new reality. April thinking something I couldn't guess at and maybe didn't want to. Me looking at a churned-up jumble of her and Dan and snow blowers and her and wandering hands and her.

"Welcome" said the first sign by Molloy's driveway. Welcome to Lakeside. I walked the women to the snow-covered doorstep, made sure they were safely in, and then I asked Helen for Matt's medication.

What for? It was a question in April's eyes but she was smart enough not to say it out loud.

"Oh dear," said Helen, still in a wooly muddle of shock. "In my coat? Oh. No. Yes, here. In my purse. I put them in my purse because you can't miss a dose of these things. He's such a fuss about bulges in his pockets."

She handed me a bundle of white-topped plastic bottles, neatly wrapped with a rubber band, and then focussed for a minute, "Did Dr. Byrne think the prescriptions might be wrong?"

"Might be. It's something to test."

"And how long till you know?" asked April.

"At least a week."

• • •

"So what was going on at this party?" Carr asked me. He had his big feet on his desk, leaned way back in his swivel chair, and he looked like a barn cat with a clear line on his prey.

"It was a Burns Night. You know, Scottish stuff. Bagpipes. Food. Drink." I did my best to leave out the versifying but unfortunately Carr had sent someone over to rescue Matt's dinner plate and that mouse was already out of the bag.

"And you were reading poetry," said my sergeant, with a studiously straight face above the standard issue OPP moustache.

"Not me." Which was true. Technically.

He let it ride for now, but I knew a tactical retreat when I saw one.

Carr decided, thankfully, that we didn't need to talk to everyone who'd been there. "Useless anyway. No worse witness than a person at a party. No clue where they were or what they were doing themselves, any given time, much less what the other guy was up to." Plus it would get the whole town talking, probably too soon.

But, based on what I'd told him, he said we better look at Dan and Helen and April.

"I'll take the women," He announced. "You take LeBlanc. And don't go soft because he drove you to school when you wore short pants."

I thought that was unfair when I'd given him every last detail I had. Right over the sick feeling it gave me to do it. Right down to April dishing out the dinner, April cornered by that lout in the hall. Everything she'd said or indicated about his behaviour, up to and including asking how long it would take to have the test results.

"You think she'll do a runner?"

I shrugged. You're the sergeant I thought. At least some of the dirty work should be for you.

• • •

The first person to admit that Constable T. Aardehuis is not much at the art of the suspect interview would be me. There's a fakery about it I can't stand. "The interviewee will be anxious to please; this natural response to the stress of police scrutiny may be used to your advantage. Build on simple positive responses elicited in the early stages of the interview, gradually leading the suspect closer to agreement with the interviewer's assessment of transpired events." That kind of B.S.

But I did my best with Dan. We talked for hours about his old grievance with the dead man. The lies and insults he'd suffered, right up to Burns Night. I did the buddy thing. "The suspect may cooperate willingly if the interviewer establishes a sense of friendship or camaraderie. I did the soft sell. Suggesting that the crime was in someways justified by circumstance may provoke agreement." I even tried the full scam. "Suggesting that evidence has been obtained which confirms guilt may increase the suspect's cooperation." I told him someone had seen him put something onto Matt's plate.

"Well they seen wrong," he said.

All I had left was the heavy, and I just couldn't see myself pounding the table while Dan sat there with his arms folded, looking at me like I'd lost my mind.

I sent him home and told him to stick around. He let me know there were no hard feelings by asking about my Mom and Dad.

Carr, on the other hand, had a pit bull reputation as an interviewer. Bite hard and don't let go. He spent two hours with Helen, four with April. I was never less happy with my job than the few minutes she took to walk out of the office. There was a bruised look about her eyes, but she looked straight ahead. Head up. Past my desk and straight to the door like she had to get out before the poison of my chosen world made her sick.

"I don't know," said Carr when she'd gone. "Maybe it's nothing after all. Autopsy said he just had a heart attack. Pure and simple. No strange chemicals in him either. I think you and your doctor might just have made a lot of trouble for nothing."

April wouldn't look at me at the funeral either, though Helen did.

"I appreciate you coming, Tony," she said afterward at the tea in the church basement. I could tell she meant it. "It was a lovely service wasn't it? And so many people came out."

Of course I said yes. It was better than he deserved and most of the people had likely come out for her sake. But she seemed to take a lot of comfort from the idea that Matt hadn't been stinted in his send off, and who with half a heart could deny her?

"It was nice, Helen. Fine music, too."

"April arranged all that." She turned to find her but April had taken herself off to the other side of the hall.

So Matt was waked and buried before we got the test results back. The report said there was nothing wrong with the bits of haggis and turnips left on the plate decorated with a racing wolf. But there was nothing but baking powder in two out of three of those red, orange and white capsules.

· · ·

It took a little wrangling with the Crown to figure out what charge we might be looking at. He didn't think we'd get murder. After all, it wasn't like Matt had been poisoned. But he changed his mind after he talked to John Byrne.

He said, "You never stop taking beta blockers abruptly. Absolutely not. Unless you want to send the heart into overdrive."

So Matt Molloy did die of a heart attack, pure and simple. Confirmed by autopsy. Killed with his own disease. Brilliant. It narrowed us down to the two who had lived with him, the two who'd had access to those pills.

All the way out to Molloy's Bed & Breakfast I thought of all the other jobs I might have done. Dairy farming with my dad. Shoe salesman. Even typing teacher didn't look so bad now.

And then we found Helen had left for the border less than half an hour before.

"She was going to take a slow drive down south" said April, looking confused. "Why? I thought the autopsy laid all that to rest?"

Carr took her down to the detachment for another round of interviews. I called all the border points and less than an hour later I picked Helen up where she'd been stopped at the St. Lawrence Bridge.

When I got there she was sitting on a chair in the Customs room, drinking coffee and chatting with the staff. They were swapping tips for the best motels on the trek down to Florida, but she didn't seem surprised when I said I'd like her to come back with me.

"There was something wrong with Matt's pills," I told her. "We need to talk about it."

"Do I have to?" she asked, a smart question. She didn't, not unless I arrested her.

I tried another tack. "Sergeant Carr has April at the detachment for more questioning."

Helen's blue attentive eyes searched mine. "He thinks she did it? Tampered with those pills?"

I nodded.

She led the way to the cruiser.

● ● ●

"She killed him because he wouldn't take her to Florida?" I tried to put this idea together with my picture of Helen Molloy and it just wouldn't work.

"It's a bit more complicated than that." said the sergeant, looking full of expert knowledge. "Like married life always is."

I didn't want to listen to the subtleties of matrimony as expounded by Sergeant Carr, but it was looking like I had no choice.

"The way I see it, she intended to be a good wife to him as long as he was around. Tampering with the medication wasn't necessarily killing him; it was just pulling an ace out of the deck."

"She didn't say any of that?"

"No. But her fingerprints are all over the bottle, all over the pills. Him being an insurance broker she's now rolling in money. And she'd heard the doctor's warning not to go off the pills abruptly. Motive. Means. Opportunity."

He paused to let it sink in before continuing. "The thing is, I think she just got tired of waiting for him to die. He kept going on about dying, all the while refusing to go on with their old life. No trips. No theatre subscription. When he wouldn't even go to the casino she must have got really scared."

"She killed him because he wouldn't go to the theatre?"

"No!" he exploded. "That was just, like, symbolic."

"I had no idea you could think like that."

He grinned. "You should talk. What was it you were going to read at that party?"

"You still think wives are such a good idea?" I said, to shut him up.

• • •

Sergeant Carr arrested Helen Molloy that afternoon and she spent that night in the cells waiting for a bail hearing. And that would have been that except the next morning my breakfast at the **Two x Four Diner** was interrupted by April sliding into the chair across from me.

She looked great. Slim as the wind in black turtleneck and jeans, tousled dark hair, brown eyes glaring at me. I looked closer and she looked exhausted. And mad.

"Helen wouldn't do that," she said, getting right down to business. "She loved the creep. Made him breakfast in bed, if you can believe it. Never let him miss a dose of his medicine. Told him 10 times that day to quit clearing the snow, that she'd take over."

I wanted to tell her I agreed.

I said, "Can't discuss it."

"I don't want to discuss." she said. "I want you to look at other possibilities."

Laurie came out from behind the counter and carefully placed a cup of coffee at April's elbow. Taking her time. Dropping two creamers and sugar packets and spoon onto the saucer like the silence she wanted to end. When she finally slopped off I said, "What other possibilities? There was you and her in the house. You surrendering?"

Not that, I thought. Please not that.

She shook her head, exasperated. "Helen. Me. And Matt. He was there too."

She had the least cluttered eyes of any woman I'd ever seen. She looked at you straight on, no wavering. "You're saying he messed up his own pills?"

"Just as believable as Helen doing it. He's the one who went on about wanting to die."

I thought about it. About a man giving up on the pleasures of life. Going on at the party about the odds of dying. Drinking when the doctor had told him not to. Even that speeding ticket. "How could you ever prove he did it himself?"

Finally, she smiled. "You're the cop. You figure it out." Then she really smiled. "Maybe you'll find his fingerprints on the baking powder box, and I never saw that guy cook a thing the whole time I lived there."

Half an hour later I figured it out sitting on the edge of Matt and Helen's bed, skimming books on the bedside table that looked like the reading of a man who wanted to stay alive. But that wasn't what he'd been studying.

In the *Layman's Guide to Heart Disease*, Matt, who'd calculated the probabilities all his life, had underlined the passage that told him patients who didn't take beta blockers were 43 per cent more likely to die within two years of their first heart attack.

The same green ink underscored the information on side effects in *An Encyclopaedia of Heart Medications*. Beside possible sexual dysfunction he'd scribbled in firm upper case letters: "NO DAMN WAY".

Another circled quote: "Do not stop taking this medicine on your own. Missing a dose by a few hours is usually not a major concern — missing several can kill you." Alongside he'd scribbled, "Russian roulette. With pills."

We also found his fingerprints on the baking powder box.

• • •

The next few weeks were rather tense in the Armagh detachment. It isn't easy for a sergeant to have his homicide trashed by an underling and I did my best to keep a low profile. It wasn't hard. Molloy's death was the first serious case I'd untangled (with help) and I should have felt pumped. The weeks after Burns Night seemed as endless and grey as a long dead marriage with life. We slid towards March on the same snow we'd been looking at since Christmas, and then, one Saturday morning, Sgt. Carr and I stepped into MacNeill's Hardware.

"You seen April?" asked Howard, as the sergeant aimed for the plumbing supplies at the back.

"Nope," I said.

"Why not?"

"Hopeless case."

"Why's that?"

Did I have to spell it out? She'd helped me get Helen off the hook. After that her face took back the look she'd worn the day she walked out of Carr's office.

Then Howard's door opened and there she was.

"Hi," she said to Howard, "Where do you keep your light bulbs?"

I got a nod. This was progress.

"Hey, April," said Howard, and then a familiar look, part frustrated general, part devil, came over him.

"Tony was just saying how disappointed he was that he never got to read his poem."

She turned and actually looked at me. "Too bad his turn never came."

"Like hell," I thought.

And then a bizarre thing happened. Maybe because I couldn't believe it was as grey and hopeless as I've been led to believe. Maybe because somewhere at the back of my head a voice starts yelling, a half-garbled burr hollering, "Try at once for intimacy."

So I think, it's now or never, last chance, and I'm even aware that Sergeant Carr has drifted back up to the front of the store and I'm feeling like 100 per cent idiot but still, I say to this girl:

"Will ye go to the Indies, my Mary,
  And leave auld Scotia's shore?"

Not loud, because I'll take enough crap for this. Through five verses, some in the wrong order, but who's complaining? Not Carr. He's looking at me like I've jumped off a bridge. Not her. If I thought about what her face meant, brow furrowed like she's deep in thought or astonishment or laughter, I'd get mixed up. So I don't. I just talk straight to the end:

"I hae sworn by the Heavens to my Mary,
    I hae sworn by the Heavens to be true;
And sae may the Heavens forget me,
    When I forget my vow!"

And she says, "I don't know about the Indies, but I've got a couple of tickets to the opera."

Chances

Nothing prepares you for the way police work can go in an instant from dead boredom to heart pounding adrenalin overdose. There I was, tucked into the shadow of a 401 overpass, sipping cold coffee and feeling the stubble on my chin grow second by second. Out there in the great world, regular dispatches informed me, a child in Montreal had been stolen, a bank in Ottawa robbed by persons who left the scene in a blue van, a teenager jumped the fence at the Horizon Detention Home.

All that going on and my slice was the 401, a 2 AM boring stretch of headlights blurring toward Toronto. I opened the cruiser window to keep myself awake and wished Miss April Brown was with me so she could see how unthreatening my profession really was. My backside was getting sore from sitting so long; the rest of me was sore from her last barrage: "Cops have way too much power. You guys are the first line in the system and that's where most people get clubbed. Sometimes people just need a chance."

Give me a chance, I'd thought. What I got was a long yarn about some woman whose family had been shot to hell when the mother slapped a drunk teenager, ended up in jail, kids taken by the Children's Aid Society. "All because the first cop overreacted."

Outside, in the dark fields, winter was just retreating, leaving patches of late March snow beneath the naked clumps of wild scrub. I'd only been working on this girl since February. Not long enough to know what she meant by it all. Love of a good argument? An excuse for the coming brush-off?

God must have a sense of humour, I thought. Why else, out of all the world, would she be the one to invade me? Why was I sitting here alone, arguing with her in my head when I wished she was really here, and maybe she'd just shut up for a few minutes and something else could happen?

Then the radio spoke. "Coming your way, Tony. Cellphone report on a beige and white pickup westbound. Cut off another car with inches to spare. Thought he was really aiming for him."

I pulled off the shoulder into the oncoming stream. In the middle of the night the road from Montreal to Toronto is for trucks and the driven who'd rather miss a night's sleep than thread the daytime crush. But even in the dark between cities the 401 is a crowded road. Two lanes carrying enough traffic for three. A road ripe for close calls and loss of temper.

Headlights in the rearview mirror approached at a steady one 120 clicks. I stayed with the flow, slowing down when I could do it without peeving anyone. I wanted that beige and white pickup to catch up with me.

If he drove like he changed lanes he'd come weaving through the traffic just past Armagh. Instead, he hurled down the highway on the east side of town, not speeding, not weaving like a drunk. Just bulling down the road a car length off the bumper of a little black sedan, both going hands above the speed limit.

I knew the truck. It was Junior Sider's pickup from the farm beside my Dad's, a brand new Chevy with a 454 V8 engine.

I had to boot it to catch up. One-twenty, 130, 140. Even with roof lights flashing to clear the lane it took a minute to reach him and all the way I'm wondering how Junior Sider, Brethren in Christ stalwart, father of four, chicken farmer and occasional guest on the Mennonite preaching circuit can be racing down the 401 in the dead of night.

I flicked on the siren, pulled level going 160 kilometres an hour and saw that it wasn't Junior behind the wheel. It was the runaway from Horizons.

I knew Marty Finch too and his CV was nothing like Junior's. Foster home Ping-Pong ball, champion shoplifter, newly graduated, apparently, to car theft and dangerous driving. I'd liked the little smartass ever since he took the full rap for spray painting the water tower when everyone could also see a girl's hand in that artwork.

When I pulled up alongside, Marty glanced over and nodded. Not scared. Not cocky. More like, relieved. He slowed down. All the way down to a sedate 150.

The Passat didn't.

So Marty sped up again, pulled right back tight to the bumper.

Dark haired and skinny with a stud glinting in his nose, his arms held the steering wheel more like he was riding a crazy horse than driving a truck. After the one glance at me, he never took his eyes off the square butt of the little car.

Which was a VW Passat: rack-and-pinion steering, standard cruise control, 1.8 litre turbo engine. $21,000 list. I almost bought one in January and then April came to town and I thought maybe I'd save my money for settling down.

I tried to stop the Passat next. Drew alongside and looked in. Lone driver. In his 30s maybe. Clean shaven. Suit and tie. He looked across and met my eyes, glanced back at the road, in the rearview mirror, around again. Like he didn't have time to be scared; like he was just concentrating hard on staying alive.

I pulled into the lane in front of him and braked slowly, hoping to bring them both down to a speed safe enough to pull onto the shoulder. But the pickup must have bumped up too close and spooked him. The Passat swerved into the outside lane. As he flew past I caught a glimpse of him hunched forward, holding the wheel like the last rung of a broken ladder. Then saw Marty breathing down the bumper, and I followed, swerving so close in front of a semi the horn blast made my fillings hum. I settled in behind the two of them, radioed dispatch and asked for a car from the next detachment to give me a hand.

We ran down the highway like beads on a chain, the little black sedan, the pickup, my cruiser, gradually settling down, once they realized I wasn't going to try to stop them, to a steady 135. What could I do but stick close and wait for help?

"So this is what it's like, April," I thought, as we dogged the lanes and each other. "To serve and protect."

"Protecting the middle class, you mean." I could hear her loud and clear over the hum of the tires.

"And what class are you?" I asked her.

There was that smile, the teasing mouth and dark eyes that caused such trouble for my beat skipping heart.

"The class of conscience," she'd say, with a laugh at herself.

No examination of conscience needed to figure this out. Yes, Marty Finch's whole life was a fuck-up. And he was a nice kid considering the times he'd been dumped by parents, grandparents, foster parents, Children's Aid Society workers. Too bad this stunt would likely end, if he didn't get hurt, with Marty in closed custody. Kindergarten for the Millhaven bound. Too bad.

"But do you think I should let him scare that little man in the black car half to death?"

"No," she says, "But he's a person. Not a crime. Not a stat."

"Well, I'll remember that."

In the dark ahead a set of red taillights appeared, the Passat gained on another OPP cruiser, a rough voice growled over the radio, and my heart sank.

"So, Tony, what we got?" Joe Kuzyk, known in five detachments as That Jerk.

"The pickup's chasing the sedan. It's Marty Finch. Won't stop. Clipped another car earlier."

Joe Kuzyk. There was a cop for April to consider. A hard-ass who clipped handcuffs tight, a climber on the scrounge for career points, a gun collector who'd discharged his weapon more times than the Armagh detachment in its entire history.

"The kid got a gun?"

"No way. No gun."

You could almost hear the disappointment. But how could I be sure? If Marty had graduated to using a truck as a lethal weapon why wouldn't he have a gun?

I hung on to the look he'd thrown across the lane when I first pulled up alongside, that nod of recognition, the hint of relief. Like maybe he wasn't all that thrilled with what he was doing.

"Here's the drill," said Joe. "You pull alongside between the two of them. I box them in at the front. We slow to the inside shoulder, push them into the grass. Got it?"

In the slow lane I sped up till I reached the truck. This time Marty rolled down the window, tried to shout something that I couldn't, for the rush of wind, begin to hear. Whatever he was trying to tell me, I just hoped I'd get to him first.

Give him credit, the Kuzyk manoeuver worked like a charm. Out front his cruiser straddled the two lanes. We pulled down to 110, lights flashing so the traffic behind would back off. Down to 80. Sixty. Forty.

At 30, Kuzyk said, "Now slide the bugger onto the shoulder."

He didn't have to run around a car to get there first. Marty was half out the door when Joe reached him, shoved him down on the ground, face into the gravel. The boy twisted around, looking for me.

"The trunk. You've got to look in the trunk."

"Shut up!" Kuzyk's boot landed on his back.

A pickup has no trunk.

The Passat.

I swung around as the engine started, saw the black car squeeze out past Kuzyk's cruiser. Not back onto the road; across the grass median between east and westbound lanes. Little wheels bouncing on rough turf but going, slowed by the tall grass but aimed straight for the eastbound stream.

I took the truck.

After all, it was the best thing for the terrain and I knew Junior wouldn't mind. The big tires chewed up the yards but the Passat had a good head start. I thought he'd get across before me and what was in that trunk? Drugs? Weapons? If he made it he'd be into the lanes headed for Montreal and away. Him and whatever was in his 12.5 cubic metres of cargo space.

I gunned it, hoping to cut him off in the last few metres when he hit a bundle of snowfence hidden in the weeds and stopped dead.

He just waited for me. Staring straight ahead, his white shirt crisp and clean. No sweat stains. No wrinkles. I reached in, turned the engine off. Took the keys, made him get out and lie down on the ground just like Marty had.

Then I opened the trunk.

She looked small and fragile. Three years old? Five? Bare arms, long and thin, white as the cotton slip she wore, hugged tight around her knees. Eyes staring up at me, unblinking. A night breeze ruffled the strands of her long dark hair and she shivered.

She was alive.

"Not bad, dikehopper." said Joe, "Two good ones in a night. Make sure you mention me when you get your medal."

Then he sat in his cruiser with John James Duffy, who claimed he had no idea how the girl got in his trunk. Dispatch said she matched the description of the little girl gone missing in Montreal. Her name was Rosie.

I wrapped Rosie in a blanket and put her on Marty's lap. Then we sat on the tailgate of the truck and waited for the world to descend.

"You even have a license?" I asked him.

"I turn 15 today."

He grinned like a loon and told me he'd just taken the truck for the hell of it. "Spring fever, I guess." When he stopped to fill up at the self serve he'd heard sounds coming from the trunk of the car ahead of him in line. Then Duffy came out of the kiosk and he'd taken off after him.

"How'd you know it was a kid?"

"You mean I might 'a thought it was a dog or something?"

I nodded.

"Dogs don't cry for their mother."

I took a good long look at Marty Finch. If you took the stud out of his nose and another five out of his eyebrow he'd be a good looking kid with a smart snap in his eyes. Right now he was looking pleased with himself. Rosie leaned against him, head peeking out of the blankets on his shoulder.

"Did you have to clip that other car to keep up with Duffy?"

"I'm not that careless. I saw the guy had a car phone. I figured he'd get your attention." He grinned again. "Worked too."

I thought it over for a few minutes, but not too many because there weren't many to spare. Then I walked over to Joe and made him an offer.

"What do you mean, you get the kid and I get Duffy?" His narrow eyes shrunk even more as he searched for the catch.

"It's a better arrest and you can have it. Write it up however you like. Except that Marty wasn't part of it. He's out of here."

"You're letting that little shit go?"

"No. He's going back. But without a charge."

"He stole the truck first, you know. Before he decided to be a hero."

"I know that," I said. "But he deserves something. You wouldn't have your kidnapper without him."

It was a struggle for the poor guy, juggling all those heavy moral issues. Truth, justice, points on the way to promotion.

"Alright. It's a deal."

Before the next car got there Marty and the truck were gone, sent up the road to wait for me at the ramp. "If you're not there waiting," I told him, "I will break your knees."

But he was there.

I spent the rest of the night cleaning up after the kid. I met Junior Sider on his doorstep at the crack of dawn to explain where his truck had been all night. Marty was more than lucky in his victim. It only worked because Junior's the kind of guy, if you cheat him, he'll point out the mistake you made in your math. Knowing his truck had been used to rescue Rosie, he was willing to be one of the few people in the world who knew how Marty Finch spent his 15th birthday. Then I brought the kid back to Horizons where he was written down as a voluntary return instead of a car thief racing down the high road to crime.

I did my paperwork and wrote up how I'd lost the beige and white truck when I joined Kuzyk in the chase for Duffy. Then I went home, feeling more satisfied with my job than I'd done in a long time. It was just too bad it wouldn't budge our clearance rate a bit, and I couldn't tell April a damn thing about it.

For the Rain

When the call came, late on Friday afternoon, that a boy had gone missing, we were sitting around Howard's MacNeill's house. The usual suspects killing time with beer, junk food and an odd assortment of musical instruments before heading to a concert in Kingston that Howard swore was worth the $45 ticket. The usual suspects: Angus MacInnes and his girlfriend Martina. Howard. Me. And April.

April. The woman I'd been circling for four months sat on the sofa next to Howard who leaned in close to her, demonstrating how to transfer the fingering she remembered from high school flute to the chanter of his bagpipes. Me sitting there wondering if she really could be interested in him, the guy who's been a friend, a good one, for fifteen years, ever since we crashed in the Grade Nine initiation tricycle race at Armagh High School. I'd never thought someday he could be a rival.

A rival for April Brown. Not for the first time I wondered how a girl with that high colour, dark bright eyes and gypsy princess look had come by such a bland and boring last name. When she first came to town last Ootober, picking up a sick leave for a teacher at the high school, she'd had a bizarre big city haircut. The dark hair was growing out now, probably because no hairdresser in a 60 kilometre radius of Armagh could do that lawnmower look, and every few minutes her small hand pushed it back and away from a face that sometimes made me feel like the happy fiddle in "The Lark in the Clear Air"; sometimes as dark as "Wide is the Water".

For her amusement Howard launched into an old yarn about Piper Ried. "There was this highland piper captured at Culloden," he said, "So the British put him on trial for taking arms against the sovereign king."

Howard is full of these bits of historical mouldy cheese, all of which we've heard a thousand times. Angus groaned and tried to drown him out with his fiddle, but April put her hand on the strings to quiet him down, and there was the smile that made me wince.

"So his defence was that he was no treasonous rebel, he was just a musician, just playing his pipes."

"Did he get off?"

"Nope. The judge said pipes are an instrument of war. Then they hung, drawn and quartered, the poor bugger."

She laughed, a deep down laugh that set something in her free. Howard can make her laugh but with me there's always a stiffness, that distance she won't cross. But then, Howard could make the dead laugh.

He's not your type, I thought. He's big and noisy and he needs someone who can shout him down. Not like me. In spite of all appearances, girl, I'm your man. Or could be.

That was when Sergeant Carr called and broke up the gathering.

"I got a missing kid, Tony," he said. "I know you're off-duty today …"

"Never mind that," I said. "Who is it?"

"That retarded boy. The one who steals house numbers."

"Jesse Thompson? He's not retarded."

"Whatever. His mother says today was supposed to be his first day coming home from school on his own. But he didn't make it. You know this family?"

"They moved in from an old place on the Millrace. Just last month."

"Right. So he doesn't know his way around town so good. His mother's been driving around for three hours going nuts. And the weather office says there's heavy rain coming."

"You think he could have headed for the old place out there in the country?"

"That's what I was wondering."

"I'll check it out."

"That's what I was hoping. And do you think Howard would come down and help with a door-to-door?"

The music lesson ended right then. Howard put away his beloved windbag. Angus and Martina headed with him to the detachment. No one said a word about our expensive tickets. I said to April, "I'll drive you home first."

She stopped pulling on her jacket to give me a, "that's what you think, buddy," look and said, "No, I'll go with you. He's in my Grade Nine English. If we find him it might help that he knows me."

So we got into my old car for what was supposed to be a quick drive out 15 miles to a farmhouse that's been falling down for 50 years. One glance at the least likely destination for a boy who could tell you what day of the week you were born on if supplied the date from 30 years ago, but couldn't find his way home from four blocks away.

Jesse Thompson, age fourteen, is one of those human beings you can't see without a misfired heartbeat and an involuntary "why?"

Why was a kid born like that? I don't know much about autism; just that Jesse lived in his own world, a place where flat topped number threes were so important they'd disappeared off a whole lot of houses since Joyce Thompson brought her family to town. Born with the most startling blue eyes if you could just get a look at them, because those eyes would never meet yours. Why?

The question must have driven his father nuts. As far as I knew, Michael Thompson, Jesse's dad, was long gone. Joyce had kept Jesse and her two younger kids in that collapsing farmhouse on the Millrace only as long as it took to get herself qualified as a nurse, take a job in town and move to better quarters.

As we drove out of Armagh I could see Sergeant Carr's storm moving in from the north like a gunboat. One mile out a spitting rain escalated fast into a downpour. Two miles and I would have pulled onto the shoulder if I wasn't thinking about a kid who might not know exactly where he was going trudging through the hard rain.

So we pushed on, wipers barely making a dent in the river streaming down the windshield, ventilation in my 10n-year-old Tercel failing to prevent a humidity level of 98 per cent.

"So you teach this kid." I said. It was hard to picture Jesse sitting through a class on *Twelfth Night*, harder to understand why someone would want to make him.

April nodded. "He comes with a child care worker."

"How does that go?"

"Mostly it's fine. Last month was a bit rough. Carol, that's the worker, said he was having a hard time with the move. Autistic kids like their routine and the change really threw him. A lot of the behaviours they try to keep banked down really exploded for a few weeks."

"Like?"

"The spinning thing. He's obsessed with anything he can spin." April leaned forward as she peered through the glass, hands tucked under her jeans, an odd mixture of amusement and pity and admiration in her voice. "Last week a bank of lockers came off the wall because he'd stolen all the screws. Worse is his thing with girls and their hair. He adores hair. You can turn around and find him inches behind you and he'll say, 'I love your hair. Your hair is so clean and shiny.' It really creeps the girls out."

"No kidding. That ever backfire on him?"

"What do you mean?"

"The girl gives him a push. Or her boyfriend."

"Oh. No. No, they all know him by now. Once they see it's Jesse they're pretty tolerant. I see him in the caf at lunch time. He even has a few kids to play cards with; he can score up the points faster than anyone. No sense of strategy though."

"And no one ever takes advantage?"

She shrugged. "Not that I can tell. "

"Then the world's indeed becoming a kinder gentler place."

April looked sideways at me and even with my eyes on the streaming road I could feel that sudden smile like sunshine in the cold rain, "You talk like that in the detachment?"

The detachment. There was territory I needed to avoid. That much I'd learned since she arrived. Not surprising, given that her first encounter with OPP Armagh had been across an interview table when her landlord died, suspiciously. Us treating her like a murder suspect.

But three months later, the fact that I'm a cop was still a boulder in the road. We'd had a few excursions, one or two of them ending in a few fine moments in-the-doorway-but-no-further. But whenever it seemed like we were getting close, the next thing you know we're having a tense talk about the percentage of native people in Canadian prisons. As if I had anything to do with that.

And friend Howard hadn't helped. Just by being so goddamned fun to be with. Then by coming to her rescue when she had to find a new place to live in a hurry and he dusted off the old apartment above his hardware store.

And then there was the time I flew back from an RCMP funeral in Yellowknife. When he picked me and my dress uniform up in the middle of the night at Dorval there was April in the front seat beside him.

"To keep me awake," he'd said.

Ceremony of any kind brings out the maudlin war horse in Howard. The whole drive home he pumped me relentlessly for details; how many officers, uniforms, protocols, pipes and drums, and what did they play? And did the guy leave a wife behind? Then he started on about how many cops die in the line of duty, not to mention the ones who kill themselves; the monument to dead cops on Parliament Hill. How long till this guy's name gets added? Or mine?

"Change the topic, Howard," I said finally.

At last he noticed that she hadn't said a word in 50 miles. That she sat spooked and pale, facing relentlessly out into the dark night and the fields passing by.

So I'd think, this is going nowhere. I'd stop thinking about her, or tell myself I'd stopped. But then some dumb thing would happen: Parker's horses would get on the provincial highway for the fourth time in a month. Or I'd broker a peaceful settlement between fist fighting relatives over what casket to choose at Dixon's Funeral Home. In my head I'd be talking to her, telling her all about it. Trying to get that smile out of her and spend half an hour at it before I remember I'm responsible for the native prison population and this is going nowhere.

Nowhere was the plateau we'd reached the day we drove out to look for Jesse Thompson. No sign of him along the highway. We turned north onto the Millrace, a gravel road tracking alongside a creek deepened a hundred years ago to turn a millwheel downstream. Farms on the east side of the road sat on the other side of the creek, and every driveway started with a bridge across water swollen with rainfall from the north, lapping almost level with the road and just 15 centimetres below the bridge planks. The going was even slower here, the road awash with runoff, wipers slapping back and forth to produce a second or two of vision.

This was not my end of the county but I had an idea the Thompson place was a mile or two past the first cluster of mailboxes where three houses shared a single bridge. Then a long lonely stretch of road.

"There he is,"said April.

We spotted him just as he neared the bridge. A lanky figure with spider arms and legs, wet jeans pasted to his legs, leaning forward into the rain, head bobbing with the pace he was keeping, walking hard and fast towards his old home. He heard the car coming. You could tell because he leaned farther into the rain, moved even faster, shifted into a half run toward a rusty mailbox that might have read *Thompson*, turned down the driveway and ran across the bridge.

I stopped the car and watched the red blur of his Armagh Motors jacket disappear around the back of the old brick house.

"Stay here," I said. "I'm not driving across that thing."

"He knows me," said a woman who knew her own mind as she stepped into the rain beside me.

"Alright then." But I took her hand and held it hard as we crossed the boards, my ears roaring with the sound of wind, rain, and angry water that couldn't stand confinement to such a narrow channel, and she left it there even when we were across, slogging through the mud toward the old house. An old Ontario house set well back from the road on a little rise, orange brick, gothic window in the single peak, gingerbread trim rotted and half fallen away. A pattern house you'd find on a thousand back roads, and some would even have the summer kitchen with crooked porch onto which we jumped out of the downpour. The door hung open and we stepped in. I called, "Jesse?" and April took her hand out of mine.

The silent, unlit house smelled damp and forgotten. Heavy footsteps hit the floor above us, moving from room to room. In the gloom we found the staircase, climbed up to the landing, one room left and one right. On the left a shoe came out of a closet, then a comic book, old clothes. There was Jesse crouched in the twilight, running his hands along the baseboards, looking for something with his hands.

"Hi, Jesse," said April. She squatted down to his level, talked to him like they'd met at the corner store, and I was suddenly very glad that she was there. "What are you looking for?"

"Not here," he grunted, and wiggled backward into the slightly brighter light of the bedroom, his soaking clothes covered with thick grey dust.

"Not here," he said and headed for the other bedroom, where he dove into that closet and felt along the shelves from top to bottom, top to bottom again, along the baseboards.

Whatever it was, wasn't there either. So he went back to the first closet, top to bottom, along the baseboards. Kind of ignoring us, except for saying, "not here," which might have been for us or might have been talking to himself, who could tell? Kind of just accepting that we were there, no big deal, just keep out of my way so I can run from closet to closet looking for something that's not there.

On the third pass, April stopped him. She held the soaked sleeves of his jacket, made him stand in one place and said, "Look at me, Jesse."

He didn't want to do it. The mulish look I'd seen when we tried to find out where all the missing house numbers had gone came over his long narrow face. His lips were blue and he shook with cold.

She said, "Eye contact, Jesse." So he gave in, gave her a quick glance and then away. "What is it, Jesse? What do you need to find? We can help you look."

"Dad's stuff," he said, pulling away, anxious to get on with it.

"Stuff?"

"Dad's stuff."

She let him go and he was back at it, closet to closet.

"Something got left behind when they moved?" I suggested.

She nodded, thinking. "He's soaked through. We've got to get him warmed up."

"We've got to get him back to town." I said, "His mother will be going crazy."

"My phone's in my bag. Out in the car. Why don't you let them know we're here and then we can take our time, see if we can get him dry. Find whatever he's looking for."

"All right." Smart girl, I thought.

Jesse passed again on his way back to closet number one, and she picked up some of the left-behind clothes, held them up for size, looking for something that might fit him.

"Guess we're not going to make that concert," I said.

She examined a pair of overalls, ripped knee and one of the buckles missing. "These'll do. The concert?" She smiled, then shrugged. "Real life is always more interesting than art."

"You talk like that in the staff room?" I asked.

"Just go make the call."

So I was smiling on my way down to the bridge, cold rain stinging my face, head down because night was coming in fast and it was getting hard to see the soggy ground.

I was thinking I could try to fool myself but it was just too late. No choice. She'd invaded me. All the walls down without even knowing when or why. It was just too late and it scared me more than a little how much it mattered. Then I heard the rumble that lifted my head. A roar of water, then the smash as part of a bridge from upstream crashed into Thompson's bridge, then a growling, creaking moan, followed by a great crack as the planks lifted like wings out of the water, hovered, slammed down again and floated away downstream.

Little Tercel sitting hubcap deep. On the other side.

"So how are we getting out of here?" April looked at me like it was my fault the bridge had floated away.

"We're not. Not tonight anyway."

"Can't we walk it?"

"Walk where? Chances are good the next bridge is gone too. We could go the back way to the next concession but that's two miles through the muck. In the dark." I nodded at Jesse who rocked back and forth on the bare floor, dwarfed by the huge shirt and overalls she'd found him, his lips still purple. "Look at him. You're just getting him dry. And all he had on his feet were those runners."

"But his mother ..."

"They'll figure it out when we don't come back. By morning they'll be here. Somehow."

"By morning."

I didn't think the prospect of a night alone, almost alone, with me should inspire that look. And what exactly was that look? Sadness? Panic?

"Hey, I thought real life was more interesting than art."

She looked about ready to throw Jesse's wet shoe at me; and thought better of it. Then we focussed on practicalities like staying warm.

And we turned out to be lucky because of the way Joyce Thompson had moved. The day she left the farm for good there'd been no one waiting in a moving van, ready to view with anxious pride the space she'd just cast off. Who'd want to live in a decrepit back road house with bad plumbing and a leaky roof? Joyce had left the place like you abandon a sinking ship, throwing the valuables to safety, careless about the odds and ends left behind. Not wanted on the voyage, they could rot and sink along with the old house. And who could blame her, considering this was where she'd been abandoned herself?

But her leavings were our good fortune. Rummaging through the fireplace cupboard I found matches and the cache of candles every farmhouse needs for the inevitable power failures. There was a stack of wood in the back porch so I got a fire going and parked Jesse near it. April emerged from a slip room off the kitchen with two tattered, old quilts, draped one over Jesse's shoulders so that he sat cross legged, finally peaceful, mesmerized by the flames.

"There's some raunchy-looking mattresses in there too," she said.

It felt like half a battle won, getting that boy warm and dry and settled in one place.

"Did you find what he was looking for?" I asked.

"Not yet. Don't even know what it is. 'Dad's stuff.' Whatever that is." Arms hugged around her jacket for warmth, she looked down at him with a smile that mixed affection and pity. Then she asked, "Where is his father anyway?"

"I don't know. Took off and left them, I think. Don't know the full story because it happened when I was posted up north. I think it all got to him and he just took off."

"What got to him?"

"Life. Jesse. Plus he had a little trucking business that went belly up in the recession."

She looked around the bare room, eyes moving over the stained wallpaper, the sagging floor. "So he left her here. In this dump."

"Yeah. Not fair. I guess he thought he could run from his troubles."

A defeated look took the light out of her eyes, the same shadow I'd encountered whenever the native prison population became my responsibility. "But you can't run from your troubles," she said. "He thinks he has, maybe. For a minute here or there. But you can't get away. Not like that."

Then she turned into the kitchen and started rummaging through the cupboards; holding a candle as she peered into the back of every drawer, every cupboard.

"What are you looking for?" I asked.

"Something to eat. I'm starving."

She rummaged and I watched, thinking that those jeans were a perfect fit and it was nice, the way she moved; calm and small and limber and smooth. Those jeans that made her look like a little girl and a woman at the same time.

I also thought, uneasily, how little I really knew her. What made the shadows come and go in her eyes like that? Where was she from and what troubles had she known in her short life? "You're not really from Newfoundland. Are you?" I asked.

Just that afternoon on the way to Howard's, at the Brewer's Retail counter we'd been right behind Tommy Hayes in the line. He ordered three two-fours of Blue, all the while bad-mouthing the nephews who'd come up for a visit and cleaned out his stock.

"Can't trust a Newfie anywhere near your beer," he says, which is all right because you can still hear The Rock in every word he says. So the guys behind the counter, Bryce and Ricky, play along, start in on the Newfie this and Newfie that.

"Hey, I'm surprised they knew what to do with it …"

"Yeah, how many Newfie's does it take to open a beer?

"Easy. One to hold the cap and four to turn the bottle …"

All harmless goofing around and Tommy loves it. Then from the woman beside me comes this throat clearing, "Ahem". We all turn to look at April who just looks back with a bland smile and a twinkle in her eye, and the guys shut right up. Wondering if they've crossed the political correctness line and if she's for real and what she might mean by it if she is.

Tommy's cases come rolling out of the backroom and he picks up all three of them and staggers out.

"Wellington's Iron Duke," I order.

"That stuff any good?" asks Ricky, who avoids trouble when he can.

"You're not a Newfie," says Bryce, who always meets it head-on, looking at April who grins back at him and says not a word.

They're still guessing when we leave.

Now she lifted two tins of soup triumphantly from the dark recesses of cupboard and grinned at me. "No, I am not from Newfoundland. But that was fun. Sure had those guys puzzling,"

"How do you plan to open those tins?" I asked.

"Don't you have a Swiss Army knife? What kind of a Boy Scout are you?"

"The same kind that leaves the cellphone in the car."

But we did manage to open two tins of beef vegetable soup with a hammer and a chisel I found in the woodshed, then heat them in the fireplace coals, then take turns sipping soup out of a cracked mug left beside the summer kitchen pump. For awhile all three of us sat on the mattresses I'd pulled out of the side rooms and watched the fire. Then, after a contented interlude of quarter spinning on the plank floor, Jesse lay down, curled up in his quilt, and went to sleep.

"That looks like a good idea," said April.

I pushed the other quilt across at her. A thick, plain-use blanket pieced from the scraps of old wool coats, dark marks on the surface left by use as a moving pad showing even in the flickering light. She took her shoes off, rolled up her jacket for a pillow, and said, "You ever read that short story by Thomas Raddall? It was in the Grade Twelve anthology where I went to school."

"Here too," I said. "Set in Nova Scotia. Long ago. There's a young preacher and the girl he's supposed to marry to some nasty old man and they get lost in a storm on the way to the wedding."

"That's the one."

"I liked the ending," I said. If I remembered right, in the end Kezia Barnes and her preacher decided to team up. Forever.

"Don't get any ideas.," But she smiled. "I just mean …"

I knew what she meant. There was one blanket and two of us and a few minutes later we lay together under it like Kezia Barnes and her Mr. Mears when they bundled in the bearskins to keep from freezing to death.

April faced the fire, I lay behind her, my arm around her shoulder. Too bad it was a fully clothed shoulder. Too bad the mattress was mouldy and the quilt smelled faintly of machine oil and our charge snuffled softly in his sleep just a few feet away. But being that close was nice. Made me think that maybe someday we'd get it right. It was an inspirational thought. It caused my arm to move, my hand to run down her side and up again searching, searching ... feeling her go rigid under my hand with unwelcome.

"All right. All right," I said. "Just let me know when you're ready." Which will be when hell freezes over, I thought. And then she took me by surprise.

"Tony. Not now. It's just ... it's not you ... it's just ..." Normally she was quick with her words, knew exactly what she wanted to say. Now she struggled and it almost hurt to hear her groping for the way.

"Shh," I said into the warm back of her neck. "It's okay. We'll talk about it. In the daylight."

"Across a table."

"A big one."

"Four feet across, minimum."

I could hear the smile back in her voice. Not now meant maybe sometime. Didn't it? When hell freezes over. We'd see about that.

"What are you thinking?" I asked.

"I'm thinking this whole situation is really weird."

"It's the stuff of great literature," I said. "And I'll behave. Scout's honour."

Then, to reassure her that I could think about more than the one thing, I changed the topic. "What do you think Jesse's looking for?"

"Something to do with his father. Something important to him. No matter how dumb it'll look to us. The way he goes on about it, it must have driven his mother crazy. Yapping about his dad's stuff when dad was the guy who left her here."

We were quiet for awhile, shifting a little on the mattress, trying to get comfortable without poking each other, watching the flames, watching Jesse sleep.

"Why's a kid born like that?" I said, before I realized I'd said it aloud.

"You don't stop, do you?" she said. But after awhile she went on and it wasn't what you'd expect. "Does it look that bad? He just stays in there by himself. Jesse's world. Never has to figure out who'll be there tomorrow and who won't. It doesn't look that bad to me."

She sounded so sombre I lifted on one elbow to try and read her face. Was she saying she'd been there too? But before I got there she shook herself into a smile and said, "Don't ask. Why don't you tell a joke or something. Something funny."

"Tell you something funny."

"Sure."

"Is this a test?"

"Maybe."

"Be funny. Just like that. Out of the blue."

"Oh, just give it a try."

The only bit of advice I ever got about women from my brother Mike was, when in doubt, laugh at yourself. It appeals to their compassion.

So I thought for a minute. Then I told her about the summer I was 20, home from university for the summer. That was before it became clear I wasn't going to stay on the farm with the other Aardehuis men.

"One of our cows went into labour and Mike, that's my brother, he should have been a vet, decides I need to know a thing or two about birthing calves. We have a cow in labour and he puts this rubber glove on me, goes up to my armpit. Tells me to get right in there and see if I can find the forefeet."

She listened. Waited. "Is that the funny part?"

"No, the funny part is that he forgot to tell me to get the hell out of there before she had a contraction."

Silence.

"*That*'s the funny part?"

I stuck my arm out of the blanket, pulled the shirt sleeve back and held it up to the light. "Look at this. There's still a bend in the bone. See?" I turn it left and right for effect and though actually it's perfectly straight the firelight doesn't half make it look like a crooked arm.

Silence.

I thought, "Well, I tried. "

More silence.

Then I felt it start, bubbling out from under her ribs, a giggle that wouldn't stay in there and soon she was shaking with it so I had to hold her closer just to keep her from falling apart.

I was still happy when I woke up in the grey light of dawn.

Over in the corner Jesse had thrown a thin arm out onto the floor. He lay on his back like a child, long face relaxed into a world where it didn't matter that he was the strangest bird on the wire.

Beside me the rhythm changed and April woke up. It was like holding a wild creature in your hands; warm and alive and you know if you open your hands it's gone.

So I just left my hand where it was on that fully clothed waist and amazingly, she didn't bolt. Rolled her head back far enough to see that I was awake too, turned around again and stayed there, head tucked in under my chin.

"What are you thinking?" I mumbled into her hair.

The light of a dark morning grew a few degrees brighter before she answered. "I'm thinking it's nice to be warm."

I pulled her closer, if that were possible. Turned her face toward me, tried for a kiss and succeeded, briefly. Except then she did bolt and I cursed myself for going too fast. Except that everything was too fast with her.

Next minute she was sitting up with her arms tight around her knees saying, "Why couldn't I get stuck like this with Howard?"

"Howard?"

"Damn," I thought, "Give it up. Get used to feeling like you've been hit by a truck and left to die. Damn Howard MacNeill," and then I saw that she was biting her lip, trying not to laugh.

"Yes. I wouldn't have to fend him off."

I realized, happily, that Howard wasn't a rival after all. "There must be something wrong with him." I said.

So I was in a good mood when we heard the horn blast, got up stiffly from the floor, and went out onto the porch to see the man himself and Sergeant Carr standing by the cruiser on the other side of the water.

"You guys okay?" Howard called as we came down to the bank. "Is the boy with you?"

"Yes, and, yes." The water had gone down 60 centimetres but it was still a six metre channel, running fast. We got as close as we could and held a conference across the brown stream.

"We could get some planks to throw across here," said Carr, doubtfully. "It'd take awhile. Or you could walk out to Petit's farm behind you. I can't see any other way. Nothing'll drive through that muck."

I looked at April.

"We'll walk," she said.

I nodded and called the verdict across. "Tell them to have the coffee on."

"We'll be waiting for you," said Howard.

I threw the keys to the Tercel across to him and as he turned toward it I thought to ask, "Jesse's looking for something he had from his dad. Any idea what that would be?"

"His Dad?" Howard said. Nine metres away I could read the disquiet that flitted across his face.

He gave it some thought. "They used to come into the store together. Mike would buy him screws, gears … Jesse kept them in a cloth sack, the way some kids keep their marbles. Might be that's what he's after."

They drove off and April and I went back to the house to roust our charge.

Who started right back whining about, "Dad's stuff. Had to find dad's stuff." We did another top to bottom search, this time piling every piece of junk in the house into one heap on the living room floor. Finished, the mess stood 60 centimetres high. Papers, shoes, rags, a few books, soap dish, old alarm clock, tin cup, fork, pencil stubs, collection of shiny stones that mesmerized him long enough to make me think they might distract him.

But no.

"Dad's stuff," he said, doggedly.

April looked tired. That coffee was calling me. "We'll look in the barn, Jesse," I said, "and then we're leaving."

Odd how empty the barn was after the untidy house. There we did the same search, easier because there wasn't a buckle or tool or bit of machinery anywhere. Hardly even a blade of straw. Light filtered through the slatted plank walls as we walked the loft floors, the empty stalls and turned a corner into what might once have been a tack room.

Now it stank of old blood on a chopping block and the musty dander of chicken feathers, 15 centimetres deep on the concrete floor and a pile of chicken feet mummifying in the corner.

"Yuck." said April.

But Jesse made a strangled sound and jerked over to the chopping block. A dark-blue bag lay, flattened under an axe head on the blackened top. With frantic fingers he tugged the drawstring open, dumped the contents onto the block and squatted there, rummaging through his old treasures. One by one he tried to set them spinning. But the brass circles had been smashed and bent. They wouldn't turn for him, and one by one they keeled over like dead things onto the black wood.

"Who would do such a thing?" I said.

"His mother." April spoke softly but with a dreary certainty. As if she'd been there to see it. As if she could see the woman in a rage of pain smashing the one thing she refused to take away from the sinking house, just like she could see the boy trying again and again to bring his old toys back to life.

Jesse looked like he'd just been shot; April about ready to cry.

I left them there and went back to the house, rummaged quickly through the pile on the floor, went back and they hadn't moved. April watching Jesse running the ruined pieces through his hands.

I swept the broken bits off the block and set down the old alarm clock, gave it a crack with the axe head. There were more delicate ways to do this, but I didn't have the time or the tools.

I pried off the clock back, pulled out the works, poked the pieces apart and set four shiny gears spinning on the wood. It was like watching daybreak to see Jesse sit up and brighten, to see happiness come back while he watched the circles turn and whirl. April's expression was harder to read. Half a smile, half a frown; something gentle in the dark eyes.

All she said was, "They're not going to thank you for those in the Special Needs Room." But I didn't think she minded.

We let him play with the spinners for a few minutes, then we put them in the cloth bag, tucked it safely in his pocket and steered him toward the field.

As we slogged the two kilometres over uneven furrows toward Petit's farm she looked at me more, met my eyes more. When Jesse lost a shoe in the bog we worked like an easy team; I lifted him out, she retrieved the shoe and tied it back on over his muddy sock, laughing as she wiped her hands on her jeans. No doubt at all that something had changed between us. Was it just the uneven terrain that made us bump into each other from time to time? And when I looked at her it seemed like, though her thoughts might be a thousand kilometres away, they'd taken her someplace that gave her that heart larking smile when she got back to me.

We were aiming for the Petit place, a chicken farm run by an aging Brethren in Christ couple whose kids had all gone modern, though their mother still wore her hair in a bun in one of those net things that were a common sight when I was a boy. Peter Petit was a long quiet man and his wife was short and fluffy and her coffee was good and strong. She had Howard, the sergeant, and her husband fed, and breakfast waiting for us when we finally walked into the farmyard.

It made a bit of excitement for the old couple and there was no rush to leave. Carr had called Joyce Thompson and she knew her boy was safe. We sat around the big kitchen table, welcome to eat five breakfasts to make up for the hungry night, sit there all day listening to Carr explain how many places in town they'd searched before realizing we were still gone. Then getting a call that the Millrace bridges had broken up. Howard finally noticing that the apartment lights above the store had been dark all night.

"I thought you had a phone?" he said to her.

"I left it in the car," said April.

"Yeah," he said, with a wide grin, "I bet you did that on purpose." More teasing about how we'd spent the night and good thing we'd had a chaperone, the chaperone sitting there oblivious, shovelling down plate after plate of bacon and eggs.

Then the conversation fractured on both sides of me. Howard noticed a framed bit of old writing on the wall and got up with Peter Petit to read it. Sergeant Carr and Mrs. Petit started talking about Joyce Thompson's better fortunes now that she'd moved to town. I looked across the table at April who looked tired, peaceful, and beautiful.

"It's cross-lined" said Peter, pointing out how the lines of spidery script went across the yellowed paper but also up and down through the text, "so it would weigh less and be cheaper to mail. From a relative in Yorkshire, 1835, asking for help to come to Canada."

"She's a very brave woman, is all I can say," said Margaret, "Him leaving her in that evil way."

"This is neat, Tony." Howard started to read aloud, " '… experience teaches me that things are getting worse and worse here every year, money so scare and business of every sort exceedingly bad …' "

But I was listening for the answer to Carr's next question: "What happened to him anyway? Where'd he go? Does she get support from him?"

" '… the measures brought in by our present Tory ministry are not at all calculated to benefit the working classes …' "

Mrs. Petit sat back in astonishment. "Support? Don't you know that wicked, cowardly man killed himself. Went into that barn one day and hung himself from a beam."

" '… Things here are in an awful state; people are literally dying for want of food and I have resolved to come …' "

"He went into the barn and hung himself on a beam." At the sound of that, April's hand, reaching across the table to take Jesse's plate stopped, suspended, frozen in shock, a bird folded into origami and hung on a string. The moment turned and she bent her head to hide eyes all at once wide open and bruised and suddenly all the birds were spinning in my brain: the pale face turned away when Howard yapped about cops who killed themselves. A voice in the dark admiring the safety of Jesse's world. How she understood how a woman left behind could smash and destroy, understood before she'd even heard the last bit of the story. The last bit about a man who hung himself from a barn beam.

The moment turned again and April took Jesse's plate, gave him more toast, without skipping another beat said, "You better stop after this, Jesse, or you'll make yourself sick. I think I'll see if I can clean off those boots."

Sergeant Carr addressed the question of the likelihood of Joyce Thompson getting any life insurance. April stood up, walked to the door, and went out onto the porch.

Where I found her, arms hugged tight around each other, leaning against the porch post like it was the last prop left in the world. I thought I could do better than that and put my arms around her and she was where she belonged. Stiff at first and unbending, then warm and easy in my arms.

After awhile she said, "I'll tell you about it. But not now. Later."

"Soon."

So that night we went out for dinner together and talked for four hours without saying one word about the past. We discussed books and films and the sorry state of the health care system. She told me about the thesis she planned to write (Anthony Trollope and Comic Pleasure). I told her about the house I intended, someday, to build (post-and-beam). That night we left the highway and took the slow road home along the lake where the waves rippled like silver on the stones. That night we went home to her apartment and, finally, we got it right. Very right, and the world and the night and the walls between us just disappeared and there was nothing left but us, together.

It wasn't till much later when she lay in the dark with her head on my shoulder and her small arm across my chest that she started talking.

"When I was in second year, I met a grad student. His name was Greg Brown and he was working on the metaphysical poets. He didn't want to just live together, he insisted on getting married. So we did. And it was okay. I thought it was okay. He was finishing his doctorate. He had a short-term contract offer from UBC. He did his defence and I had a party for him. A surprise so it wouldn't make him nervous. Maybe it was the surprise. I went to class the next day and when I came home — home was the married students' residence — he'd hung himself. From the light fixture. Just inside the door of the apartment."

The bastard, I thought. So that was what she'd see when she come home? So she had to remember that ever time she opened a door?

"The thing is, Tony," she said, staring up into the dark, "I lived with him and ate with him and slept beside him for three years and I didn't have a clue."

"So it makes it hard to try again."

"Yes."

There are some moments so full they spill over into your whole life. Just then I felt like I knew every drop in the glass, who she was and where I wanted her to be, right there with me and how much I wanted her to want that too.

"But it's worth the risk, April."

"Is it?" There was still a twist of fear in her voice.

"Definitely worth it." I said, then she turned toward me and I kissed her and it might have been true and it might have been wishful thinking that the shadow in her eyes was already half gone.

From that apartment above MacNeill's Hardware you can hear every bell in Armagh banging away on a Sunday morning. The Catholics were first at 7:45, summoning the faithful to the early mass where you'd find my parents. April must have been used to it because she just snuggled deeper down under the covers. Then the fire hall clock struck the hour, then the half hour and at 8:30 I gave up. Pulled on my clothes, searched out the fixings for coffee and went down to get the *Kingston Whig-Standard* from the box on the sidewalk.

Ten minutes later I was back beside her, except then St. Mark's Anglican started clamouring and April sat up, and said, "Damn."

"Pretend you don't hear it," I said.

"Can't. It's the fourth Sunday. Sung service and I'm the only alto." She transformed herself into a fully put together woman in about two minutes and paused just long enough to kiss me on her way out.

"Don't you have to go to confession first?" I said.

"You're the Catholic. You can go for both of us."

"I'm a Catholic?" It was true, but I never did anything about it, not unless my mother looked cross-eyed at me long enough at Christmas and Easter.

"I've done my research," she grinned. Then she got serious. "Will you be here when I get back?"

"For sure."

She left and I spent the next contented half hour beside the warm space she'd left behind, drinking coffee and rustling pages through the events and non-events called the news. Murder, war and general mayhem.

But the sidebar I lingered over longest was the small bit under the heading:

FLOODING CLOSES ROADS

Heavy rains deluged Eastern Ontario Friday night.
Environment Canada reports that 75 mm of rain drenched
some areas in less than two hours, leading to the flooding of

creeks and rivers and the washout of several bridges near Armagh.

I thought about how much difference a bridge could make. How if that one hadn't floated away we'd still be two twigs in the stream, colliding and separating in the current of life. Except we weren't, because the rain fell and a bridge broke and forced us to hold each other to stay warm.

And I thought if I were going to break down and say a prayer for anything it would be for that. It would be thank you. Thanks for the rain.

A Selection of Our Titles in Print

www.brokenjaw.com hosts our current catalogue including book prices, submissions guidelines, Poets' Corner Award guidelines, booktrade sales representation, trade sale terms and distribution information. Directly from us, all individual orders must be prepaid. All Canadian orders must add 7% GST/HST (CCRA Number: 892667403RT0001).
Broken Jaw Press Inc., Box 596 Stn A, Fredericton NB E3B 5A6, Canada